"Josie LeClaire. I'm not a man to go for a secret fling. I want more."

A silly little squeak escaped her, and she asked again, "More?"

He gazed into her eyes, his focus unwavering. "I trust you, Josie. I like you so much. And I can't stop wanting you all the time. No, I can't offer you love, whatever that really is, but you said you didn't want it. And I swear to you that I will give you everything else. Everything—and in return, I would want the same from you. Your loyalty, your trust, your hand in mine for as long as we're both breathing. A good life, the kind of life we both want. A partnership of equals, you and me."

"You're asking me to—"

"Marry me, Josie. Please make me happier than I ever thought I could be again. Say you'll be my wife."

Oh, sweet Lord.

It all sounded so good, Miles kneeling in front of her, holding up the perfect ring, offering all the things she'd stopped hoping for—a fine life with the right man. She could have all that with him.

Everything but...

Love.

Dear Reader,

I do love a boy-next-door story. Especially one with a baby and a purely "practical" marriage that ends up being so much more.

Farmer and veterinarian Josie LeClaire has not been lucky in love. But she does want a family, so she chose a reputable sperm bank and had intrauterine insemination. Her son is due in three weeks. Though Josie lives and works at the family farm alone now, her two half sisters and beloved aunt will be coming home to support her through the birth and the first weeks of her new motherhood. It's all going to be fine. Or so she keeps telling herself...

Josie's neighbor, fellow farmer Miles Halstead, lives less than a mile away from her. She's known Miles all her life, though never all that well. A widower with two teenage daughters, Miles has always been a private sort of man—even more so since the sudden death of his wife three years ago.

Under ordinary circumstances, Miles and Josie might have lived their whole lives on neighboring farms and never discovered how very much they have in common or how beautifully their two lives might intertwine. Fortunately for them, though, a snowstorm, a disconnected landline and a lost cell phone are about to change everything. After all, Miles is a guy a woman can count on when things go sideways—and Josie is about to learn that sometimes the man you've given up searching for has been right next door the whole time.

Happy reading, everyone.

Christine

First Comes Baby...

———

CHRISTINE RIMMER

HARLEQUIN
SPECIAL
EDITION

HARLEQUIN®
SPECIAL EDITION™

Recycling programs
for this product may
not exist in your area.

ISBN-13: 978-1-335-40840-2

First Comes Baby...

Copyright © 2022 by Christine Rimmer

Harlequin Enterprises ULC
22 Adelaide St. West, 41st Floor
Toronto, Ontario M5H 4E3, Canada
www.Harlequin.com

Printed in U.S.A.

Christine Rimmer came to her profession the long way around. She tried everything from acting to teaching to telephone sales. Now she's finally found work that suits her perfectly. She insists she never had a problem keeping a job—she was merely gaining "life experience" for her future as a novelist. Christine lives with her family in Oregon. Visit her at christinerimmer.com.

Books by Christine Rimmer

Harlequin Special Edition

Wild Rose Sisters

The Father of Her Sons

The Bravos of Valentine Bay

A Husband She Couldn't Forget
The Right Reason to Marry
Their Secret Summer Family
Home for the Baby's Sake
A Temporary Christmas Arrangement
The Last One Home

Montana Mavericks: What Happened to Beatrix?

In Search of the Long-Lost Maverick

Montana Mavericks: Six Brides for Six Brothers

Her Favorite Maverick

Montana Mavericks: The Lonelyhearts Ranch

A Maverick to (Re)Marry

Visit the Author Profile page
at Harlequin.com for more titles.

Stephen King once said,
"To write is human. To edit is divine."
So this one's for my editor,
the divine Gail Chasan,
who is always in my corner
and helps me make every book the best it can be.

Chapter One

Yanked from a deep sleep, Miles Halstead popped straight up in bed. A dog barked nearby—his border collie, Bruce.

"What the…?" Miles flipped on the bedside light. On alert at the door to the front hall, Bruce whined. Ears cocked, he waited, quivering, for Miles's command.

"Sit," said Miles. "Quiet."

Bruce dropped to his haunches and stayed there.

Miles blinked away the last cobwebs of sleep. He'd heard noises, hadn't he? Loud noises…and not just Bruce barking.

Miles grabbed for his phone. The screen lit up—3:10 a.m.—as the doorbell rang twice. Rapid-fire knocking followed.

Bruce whined again.

"Bed," he said to the dog. Bruce was a great guy. He trotted right over to his bed in the corner, got in and curled up with his nose on his paws.

Shoving back the covers, Miles grabbed for his jeans. He yanked them on and then stuck his feet into fleece-lined slippers. He was pulling his sweatshirt on over his head as he emerged from the bedroom into the foyer.

Once at the front door, he hesitated.

Realistically, the chances of some bad actor standing on the porch with mayhem on his mind were practically nil. Miles's nearby hometown of Heartwood, Oregon, had very little violent crime. Here at Halstead Farm, they'd never had a break-in—not once in all of Miles's thirty-nine years.

Then again, a man never knew when trouble might come for him. Miles had done three tours in Afghanistan back in the day. His time in the Middle East had taught him that he couldn't be too careful.

Flipping on the porch light, he peered out the beveled-glass windows that decorated the top of the door. The wide porch, with its natural stone pillars topped by boxy, Craftsman-style columns, appeared deserted. Beyond the porch roof, snow drifted lazily to the ground.

"Miles!" a woman's desperate voice shouted from below his line of sight on the other side of the door. "Hello! Are you in there…?" The question trailed off on a groan and a single hard knock followed.

So, then. Probably not a home invasion.

Miles slammed back the dead bolt and flung the door wide to find his neighbor, Josie LeClaire, crouched below him right there on the welcome mat. Josie lived and worked on Wild Rose Farm, which bordered Miles's farm. He stared down at her in disbelief. She had her head tipped low. Both hands clutched her very pregnant belly.

"Finally!" Tossing back her long, curly hair, she glared up at him, her pretty face sheened with sweat in spite of the cold. The smattering of freckles across the light brown skin of her cheeks stood out in sharp relief. "I thought you'd never open up."

"I'm sorry." He dropped to a crouch beside her. "Sometimes I'm overly cautious."

She scoffed, "You think?" But then, with a sigh, she patted his hand. "It's okay, Miles. You're here now and I'm grateful—and I really need a ride to Heartwood Memorial to have this baby."

A glance at his gravel driveway showed no sign of a vehicle. "You *walked* here?"

"I was afraid to drive." She stuck out her strong chin at him. "And please don't look at me like that. Yes, I walked. It's less than a mile from my house to yours."

He pressed his lips together to keep from asking why she hadn't just called someone.

Apparently, Josie guessed what he was thinking. Flipping her hair back again, she blew out both cheeks with an impatient breath. "Okay, fine. It's like this. I lost my phone somewhere and I had no way to call anyone because a month ago I decided to save money by disconnecting the farm's landline and having it rerouted to my cell. Not the most brilliant decision, I see that now." She was shivering.

He needed to get her inside. "Come on in the house. It's got to be twenty degrees out here and you shouldn't—"

"Miles!" she cried as she manacled his wrist with one hand. With the other, she flipped all that misbehaving hair back from her flushed face again. "Contraction," she croaked at him. "Just… let me get through it." Her full mouth had pinched tight. "And don't you dare leave me, okay?"

"I'm right here, going nowhere—breathe." Miles had not only delivered calves, attended the births of more than one foal and helped shepherd a number of other four-legged creatures into the world, but he'd also coached his wife through the deliveries of his two daughters. Both times, he'd done his best to provide the mother of his children with whatever she needed, including support and encouragement. "Just breathe."

"Breathe," Josie repeated, her gaze locked on his face.

"That's it. Slow. Steady." He spoke gently, quietly. "Nice and calm..." He matched his breathing to hers. The seconds ticked by. Finally, the contraction reached its peak and faded off.

"Ashley and Hazel?" she panted

"In town at my mom's for the weekend. Let's get you inside..." He got his arm around her again and tried to urge her upright.

She balked. "Miles. You're not listening. I need to get to the hospital. Will you please drive me there?"

"I don't know if that's a good idea."

Clearly doing her best not to yell at him, she drew in a slow, careful breath through her nose. It didn't work. She ended up screeching, "Miles! Will you do it, or won't you?"

"Josie," he soothed. "Come on now, don't get yourself worked up. Take it easy. Remember to breathe, okay?"

"*Get* myself worked up? I'm already worked up. Nothing's going as planned. It's a mess, Miles." She forked her fingers through her hair again. "A complete mess."

"Are you bleeding?"

"What? No."

"Did your water break?"

"Uh, no. Not yet..."

"Well, I really do think you need to come inside. We'll get hold of your doctor. Everything will be fine."

With a groan, she started massaging her temples. "I don't get it. Why won't you listen to me?"

"Because it's snowing, and I think you should talk to your doctor first."

She narrowed her eyes at him. "Miles. I have to ask. Who made you the expert here?"

"Well, I wouldn't call myself an expert. But I did deliver Ashley on the side of the road about three hours after Fiona went into labor."

"Wow," Josie said softly.

"Yeah. It was pretty scary..." His older daughter had been born in the cab of a 1986 F-150 pickup halfway to the hospital. When he thought back to that night, he could still hear Fiona's screams of pain and terror. In the end, Ashley came out screaming as loud as her mother. At the sight of the tiny girl, Fiona had stopped shrieking, demanded that he hand over her baby and then cried with sheer joy.

It had all turned out fine. Mother and daughter came through the birth just great. That night, he'd been the happiest man alive...

"Miles?" Josie was staring at him, worry crunching her eyebrows together. "Are you all right?"

He pushed thoughts of Fiona and her betrayals from his mind to focus on the pregnant woman crouched beside him now.

Josie gasped as another contraction took her. She moaned and panted. He did his part and talked her through it.

"I want to push," she wailed. "I shouldn't want to push. Not yet. It's too soon to push…"

Miles made soothing noises and reminded her of her breathing until that contraction finally crested and passed, at which point he accepted that he needed to stop arguing with her. "Okay, how about this? I really don't feel right about driving you, but let me get my phone and I'll call you an ambulance."

"Wait!" She grabbed his arm again in a death grip. "I think my water just broke. And why is it I'm getting the feeling that this baby's coming out very soon…?"

"I have that feeling, too. And it's freezing out here. Will you please come in the house?"

She wouldn't even stand up. In fact, she slapped at his hand as he tried again to help her upright. "Just give me a minute, will you?"

"It's like this," he said gently. "You're having that baby, and it's happening fast."

"It's fifteen minutes to the hospital."

"It *should* be fifteen minutes, weather permitting. But it's been snowing for hours."

"The wind's died down, though. The snow hasn't piled up much."

"That doesn't mean it's safe on the highway right now."

"I'm sure it'll be fine. Really, I..." Her voice trailed off. She blinked, spread her hands protectively over the large ball of her belly and stared down at it. He watched her face as understanding finally dawned for her.

This might be her first baby, but Josie was a farmer and a damn good veterinarian. It had taken her a while, but she was getting her body's message now.

"Oh, my god." She gaped. "You might be right. It came on so quickly. This is precipitous labor, isn't it? How can that be? First babies are supposed to be late. Labor usually takes hours and hours..."

He nodded and made all the right sympathetic sounds as he finally succeeded in getting her to her feet. "Come on. My room's right here at the front of the house..." He got her over the threshold and shoved the door shut. "This way."

In his room, he took her to the corner chair.

"I can't sit there. I'll leak all over it."

"I don't care."

"Well, I do." Panting and groaning, she tossed her shoulder bag on the chair and then dropped to a crouch under the window. "Could you get me a towel, please?"

"Absolutely." He ducked into his bathroom and grabbed one off the rack. "Here you go." She took it. "Now, just let me get the bed ready, okay? We need to make you more comfortable." He smoothed the top sheet and straightened the blankets. "I need something waterproof..."

"Shower curtain maybe?" she suggested on another groan.

"There's one in the back bathroom." He was already headed for the door.

"And more towels, Miles. Please..."

"Don't worry. I hear you. I'll get those, too."

In the bathroom off the other downstairs bedroom, he took the shower curtain off the rings as fast as he could and then raced to the utility-room cabinets for a spare top sheet and a stack of towels.

As he entered the front bedroom again, Josie announced, "I need to push, Miles. It needs to happen soon."

"A minute more." He dropped the towels on the chair next to her, spread the curtain on the bed and covered it with the sheet. "Just try to hold off until we get you up on this bed."

"I'll get on the bed myself. You call my doctor."

"What about that ambulance?"

She shook her head. "Later. Probably. Just my doctor for now. I don't know the number offhand, but her name is Contreras—Anita Contreras."

Josie had already shucked off her outerwear and most of her clothes, including a pair of shearling boots. Dressed now in a big shirt that came to midthigh and a pair of heavy socks, she grabbed another towel and climbed onto the bed. She spread out the towel, then perched on it, whipped off wet underpants and tossed them in the general direction of the rest of her discarded clothes.

Miles googled the doctor's number, made the call and got an answering service. A woman promised that Dr. Contreras would call back soon.

"The call service will contact your doctor right away," he explained to Josie as he hung up.

"Great," she said grimly. Still panting, she blew an errant coil of hair out of her eyes.

"I'm just going to go and wash my hands, Josie. I'll be right back, okay?"

"Go." She waved him away.

He scrubbed up and returned in a flash. Things got serious after that. Josie moaned, yowled and panted. Miles scrambled to obey every order she growled at him.

Between bouts of screaming and firing commands at him, Josie talked. She said a boatload of stuff she probably would never have shared with him under any other circumstances.

"I was so sure of how it would be," she moaned. "Me and my baby and Payton and Auntie M, a family of women, supporting each other, with Payton and me raising our children together." Josie was one of three half sisters, each with a different dad, all three of them raised by their Aunt Marilyn on Wild Rose Farm, where Josie lived on her own now. Until recently, Payton, the youngest sister, had lived at the farm, too, along with her preschool-age twin sons. "Now Auntie M's off in Salinas with Ernesto—" Ernesto Bezzini was Marilyn's boyfriend "—and Payton's in Seattle." Recently, Payton had married and moved north with her new husband, the father of her twins. "They'll both be here—Auntie M and Payton— on Wednesday, which is two weeks before I'm even due. This shouldn't be happening. We had it all planned..." Josie let out a wail of frustration.

And then, hardly pausing for a breath, she switched subjects.

She told him all about how she'd chosen her sperm donor, of all things. "I wanted someone smart and tall and athletic. The donor I used is six-three. He skis and runs marathons and he graduated college with a three-point-eight GPA."

Miles nodded and made encouraging noises as she babbled away. He never would have guessed that his neighbor had a sperm donor—a literal one, a man she'd chosen from a list of donors at a sperm bank, and someone she'd never actually met.

When Miles had first noticed that Josie was pregnant, he'd assumed there must be a guy in the picture, at least for the sperm donation.

He wondered if his daughters knew how Josie had gotten pregnant? He wouldn't be surprised if they did. Both of his girls liked Josie. They enjoyed hanging out with her—well, maybe not Ashley so much anymore. His older daughter was too busy with her friends to have much interest in anyone out of high school. But Hazel, who was thirteen now, still loved helping Josie care for the various injured and ill animals she was always nursing back to health in an old barn at Wild Rose.

Miles could easily imagine Josie mentioning how she'd chosen to become pregnant to one or both of his girls. That didn't mean his daughters would have shared the information with him. They tended to be reluctant to discuss anything remotely sexual with him. He understood their hesitance about such subjects and realized he probably should try harder to get them to open up about that stuff with him.

But discussing reproduction with his daughters made him at least as uncomfortable as it seemed to make them. He'd gotten through the basic talks well enough—how babies are made, how protection is necessary each and every time.

That was pretty much as far as it went.

Josie kept talking. "Being a single mom made so much sense in theory, you know? But the closer I got to my due date, the more I wondered what I thought I was doing. Seriously, whoever said I was qualified to take care of a newborn human?"

He fed her ice chips, wiped her face with a cool cloth and said what he figured she needed to hear, that she would be a great mom, the best mom ever in the history of moms. "My girls think the world of you, Josie. You're helpful, you're kind and you care."

"But can I *do* this?" Josie asked, her voice full of emotion. "Can I make it on my own at the farm with a baby to look after?"

"Of course, you can."

All at once, she was crying. Tears streamed down her face. "I just…don't feel prepared. I had to take maternity leave from the animal clinic. I told them I needed a few months off. It was just too much, with the baby coming and the farm to take care of." Josie had been on call for the clinic. She treated livestock and pets at all the local farms—Halstead Farm included. "I'm in over my head, not ready, not up for this, no!"

Miles's phone rang. It was Josie's ob-gyn. He felt infinite gratitude to Dr. Contreras for choosing that moment to return his call. His neighbor could use a distraction. "It's your doctor."

"At last." Josie sniffed and swiped the tears away with the back of her hand. "Would you put her on speaker, please?"

Miles punched the speaker icon. "You want me here or...?"

"Just don't go far," she said.

He handed over his cell. "I'll take Bruce out for a minute."

Josie nodded as the doctor started talking. Miles clicked his tongue at the dog, who jumped up and led the way.

When they came back in, Bruce went to the kitchen, probably in search of his water bowl.

In the bedroom, Dr. Contreras seemed to be wrapping up the call. "You're doing great, Josie. You and your baby are going to be fine. As soon as I say goodbye, I will call you an ambulance. They should be there shortly. They'll take good care of you and bring you to the hospital, where I will be waiting for you."

"But I, um..."

"Yes?"

Josie seemed to have no clue of what to say next. She looked at Miles for help. Pasting on an understanding expression was the best he could do. Josie's shoulders sagged. "Never mind," she said to her doctor. "Thanks. I'll see you at the hospital."

"Excellent," Dr. Contreras said firmly. "Just

keep on as you have been. I'll need your neighbor's address."

Miles rattled it off.

"Got it," the doctor said. With a cheerful "I'll see you at Heartwood Memorial," she ended the call.

For a moment, Josie stared blankly into the middle distance. "She had me check my own dilation and effacement. We're close, Miles. She says we're doing great."

"You bet we are," Miles agreed with all the enthusiasm he could muster.

"Here you go." She handed him back his phone.

He stuck it in a pocket and picked up the bowl with the ice chips in it. Not all of it had melted yet. "How about more ice chips?"

Josie grabbed his arm for the umpteenth time. "I'm already in over my head with work at the farm. What if I can't do this at all? What if I crash and burn and my baby suffers and grows up to hate me?"

Miles reassured her some more that she could do it, that all would be well, that his girls adored her and so would her baby and he would be right next door, ready to help out whenever she needed him.

"But my baby's a boy and boys aren't girls!" she moaned.

"Josie. Come on now. Think about it. You

looked after Payton's boys all the time when they still lived at the farm, didn't you?"

"You're right," she grudgingly agreed.

"Open up." He fed her a spoonful of watery ice.

She sucked and swallowed. "I did watch my nephews all the time. I miss Penn and Bailey so much! And maybe you're right and it will all be fine. Maybe I'll manage after all, raising a boy..." She burst into tears and started in all over again, bemoaning her lost phone and her sister and aunt who weren't here when she needed them.

Miles repeated the soothing things he'd already said: that she would be fine, the phone would turn up and she would be a good mom. A terrific mom. The best mom ever.

"Not convinced," she replied mournfully. "But I appreciate all your efforts to ease my mind. You're a good man, Miles Halstead—somewhat clueless, it's true, but nobody's perfect."

Ten minutes later, she was screaming, her shirt pulled up above her breasts, all modesty long gone.

The baby's head crowned. With the next push, a scrunched-up little face appeared.

Once both shoulders had emerged, it was over in seconds. The red-faced, wailing baby boy slid from his mother's body and straight into Miles's waiting arms.

"My baby." Tears streamed down Josie's cheeks. "My baby's here…"

Miles did a quick inventory of the sticky little guy. He looked fine and had all his fingers and toes. Sounded fine, too, with that loud, furious cry at being suddenly ejected into the big, wide world.

Over the baby's cries, he heard the ambulance in the distance, the siren blaring, growing louder.

"About time," Josie muttered. Lights flashed in the front window as the ambulance pulled up. The noise and sudden brightness startled the tiny boy. He let out a loud grunt of surprise and his eyes popped open in his red, contorted face.

"Well, look at you." Miles couldn't help but smile as he and Josie's son stared at each other. Outside, the blaring siren stopped.

"Is he okay?" Josie asked in a tired voice.

"He looks great to me." Careful of the still-connected umbilical cord, Miles transferred the baby to his mother's waiting arms.

"Hello, sweetheart." She cradled his gooey body against her chest. "I'm so glad you're here." She seemed composed now, though the tears still streamed unheeded from her eyes. Glancing up at Miles, she asked, "How can I ever thank you?"

"No thanks are needed. You know that." Awkwardly, he patted her shoulder. The doorbell rang. "I'll let them in…"

She was cooing at the baby again as he went to the door.

When he ushered the two EMTs inside, one of them asked Miles if he was the dad.

The question gave him the oddest feeling of pleasure, reminding him how happy he'd been at the births of each of his daughters. Before Fiona died, he'd still sometimes hoped they might have a boy, too.

But that was back when he had no idea that he was living a lie.

"I'm not the dad, just a neighbor." He pointed the two men toward the open bedroom door as his phone bleated in his pocket.

It was Rafe Jenks, who'd worked on Halstead Farm since Miles was in his teens. Rafe lived in a single-wide trailer near the horse pasture. "Miles, are you okay? I saw the ambulance."

Briefly, Miles explained about Josie and the baby.

"Good thing she made it to your house," said Rafe.

"Yeah."

"Give her my best, huh?"

"Will do."

As he put his phone back in his pocket, Josie caught his eye. "Could you hand me my bag?" One of the EMTs had the baby at that moment, so Josie's hands were free.

Miles grabbed the bag from the chair by the window and gave it to her. "Rafe sends good wishes."

Josie managed a weary smile. "Thank him for me."

"Will do."

She dug out her keys and then turned those amber eyes on him again. "You've been a life-saver. I hate to ask for more, but…"

"I'll look for the phone and bring it to you when I find it." He took the keys.

"Thank you." She frowned.

"What else?"

She winced. "Tink's alone in the house and I'm not sure how long I'll be at the hospital." Tinker-bell was Josie's sweet-natured Dutch shepherd.

"I'll bring her over here."

"I owe you." Josie gave him a wobbly smile. "I owe you so big."

She was still thanking him profusely as they put her in the ambulance.

Miles called Rafe as the ambulance drove away.

"Everything okay?" the older man asked.

"It's all good. Josie and the baby are on their way to Memorial." He explained about the miss-ing phone. "So I need to find it and take it to her. I shouldn't be gone long, but Josie's on her own and she might need me to stick around at Memorial. You think you could keep an eye on Tinker-bell and Bruce while I'm gone?"

"Sure, I'll get Bruce," Rafe said. "Just leave him at the house." Rafe had a key. "You bring Josie's dog to me and I'll look after her, too. It's no problem."

"Thanks. And I hate to ask..."

Rafe gave a rusty chuckle. "I'm a big boy. I can manage whatever needs doing around here on my own for a few hours. What about at Josie's place?"

"Not sure. I'll need to check with her...and on second thought, I'll just take Bruce with me to Josie's, pick up Tinkerbell and bring them both to you."

Rafe was always razzing him about how he "coddled" his dog. Miles braced himself for a teasing remark or two. But Rafe didn't get on him. "Works for me."

"Thanks, man."

"Anytime."

With Bruce panting happily on the seat beside him, Miles drove his crew cab the short distance to Josie's small house on Wild Rose Farm. The house was one of three built in a circle with a wide, sloping grassy space between them—grassy in the warmer months, anyway. Now, a blanket of fresh snow covered the ground between the three dark cottages.

When Miles mounted the steps to the porch,

Tink barked once, sharply, from inside Josie's house. He unlocked the door. She was waiting right there on the other side, a good protector.

She seemed to recognize him and gave an eager little whine when he pushed open the door.

"Tink, sit," he said, and she did.

The search for Josie's phone took about three minutes. He grabbed it and went looking for the other things Josie might need. She was a practical woman, after all, a woman who tended to plan ahead, the type to have a suitcase all packed, ready if needed for an overnight hospital stay. He found that suitcase waiting in the closet of her spare bedroom, along with a car seat and a fully stocked diaper bag. He loaded everything into his pickup on one side of the back seat, leaving the other side for Bruce. Tink, he took up front with him.

After dropping the dogs off with Rafe, Miles hit the road. The trip took fifteen minutes, exactly as Josie had said it would. Though snow had piled up on the shoulder, the road itself was clear all the way to town and also on the surface streets that led to Heartwood Memorial.

The ease of the trip had him feeling a little foolish that he hadn't taken Josie straight to the hospital when he'd found her crouched at his front door. They definitely would have made it before the baby arrived and she could have skipped the ambulance ride.

But then he grinned to himself, thinking of that moment right after the birth, when the little guy's eyes popped open, and he made that sound of complete surprise. Overall, helping Josie have her baby had made Miles feel good—helpful and competent. Needed in a way he hadn't felt in a few years now. He just really hoped the new mom and her baby had come through in good shape.

And did she have insurance? He would definitely step up and cover the cost of the ambulance ride if she didn't—after all, that she'd had to deliver her baby in his bedroom was on him.

At the small hospital, the lone woman in reception told him to have a seat in the waiting area. He'd gone to school with one of the nurses who worked there, Darlene Kent. Darlene's daughter, Aurora, was best friends with Ashley.

Miles asked for Darlene and luck was with him. Aurora's mom came on duty at six and had just arrived for her shift. Darlene vouched for him, so they let him in to visit Josie and the baby.

In Josie's room, the blackout curtains were drawn. She was sound asleep. The baby, in the hospital bassinet beside her, was sleeping, too.

The other bed was empty, so the room was really quiet.

Miles considered collecting the suitcase and

baby stuff from the truck and leaving them there. He could put her phone on the bed tray, where she would see it when she woke up. She looked so fragile, though, in the dim light that streamed in from the hallway—fragile and conked out from exhaustion.

It felt wrong to leave her and the little guy here all alone. Miles took off his heavy jacket and wool cap and dropped them on one of the guest chairs. He took the other chair just as the baby started fussing.

Jumping up again, he bent over the bassinet. "Shh, it's okay…" he whispered, and gathered the small boy in his arms. The red-faced newborn squinted up at him, his tiny, wrinkled hands curled into fists, his small mouth working. He weighed so little, like something that might blow away in a brisk wind. Had his girls ever been this small?

"How are you doing?" he asked in a whisper. "Feeling okay?"

The baby made grunting sounds. Miles thought a diaper change might be necessary.

But then the kid yawned some more and closed his eyes with a soft, contented sigh. Miles walked him back and forth for a few minutes, making certain he'd gone to sleep again.

Carefully, Miles returned the boy to the bassinet and sat down again. Just for a few minutes, he thought, in case the baby woke up again—a few minutes, and he would put on his coat and hat, bring in the baby stuff from the pickup and go home.

Chapter Two

When Miles woke, someone had opened the curtains. Gray daylight streamed in. The snow had stopped completely.

Josie, awake now, was sitting up in the hospital bed watching him. She'd corralled all that brown and gold hair in a low ponytail and she was nursing her new son. "You look beat," she said with a tired smile.

Stifling a groan, he straightened in the chair and rubbed an achy spot at the back of his neck. "I'm fine. I sat down for a minute and…"

"No need to explain." She adjusted the blanket

around the baby's face, and asked hopefully, "Any luck finding my phone?"

"As a matter of fact..." He rose, picked up his jacket from the other chair and got her iPhone from the inside pocket. Her eyes lit up. He set the phone on the bed table, within her reach. "Here you go."

She gazed up at him like he'd brought her the moon. "Where was it?"

"In the fridge."

She shook her head in disbelief. "How did you ever know to look there?"

"My mom left hers in the fridge once, so it was the second place I checked after the sofa cushions."

That had her tipping her head back and groaning at the ceiling. "I'm definitely hooking up that landline again." In her arms, the baby, sound asleep now, sighed and let go of her breast.

Miles turned away and went back to his chair. When he sat down and faced her again, she'd readjusted her hospital gown. The baby slept on.

He volunteered, "I have your car seat, suitcase and diaper bag out in my truck."

She shook her head in a musing sort of way. "Miles Halstead, you're a true hero."

He snorted out a tired laugh and teased, "You should probably name him after me."

"Too late." She glanced down at the conked-out

baby, her smile turning tender as she brushed a light finger across the plump curve of his cheek. "I've already named him David. After my father."

"I don't think I've ever met your dad."

That brought a whole new kind of smile from her, one with a slight note of sadness. "He died when I was a year old."

"Sorry to hear that…" Miles thought of his own father, who'd been a great dad and a wonderful grandpa, too. Miles Sr. had died five years before. He and Miles's mom had lived in town for several years by then—when Miles married Fiona, his parents had turned the farm over to him and moved to Heartwood.

Josie gave a one-shouldered shrug. "He was a good man, my dad—a soldier. His dad, my grandfather, was Haitian by birth. My dad's mom was raised on a Nebraska farm. My dad grew up in Miami. He joined the army at eighteen and was killed in El Salvador before he turned twenty-one. He met my mom on his first leave when he decided to see the West Coast. He was still just eighteen and she was in her twenties. He used to send me letters, even though I was only a baby, way too young to read them…" She fell silent, a thoughtful expression on her face.

And then she gave a small, wry laugh. "Surprisingly, my mother, who was not the kind of woman to save mementos for her children, actually did save those letters for me. She never married my dad, but she did give me his last name. I still have the letters, along with my dad's flag and his dog tags." She looked up from the baby and into his eyes. "And I know, I know. Way more information than you wanted or needed."

He held her gaze and said honestly, "Not what I was thinking at all."

"Right."

"I was thinking that your dad sounds like a fine man."

"You were, huh?"

"I was."

"You would be correct about that." Beneath her freckles, her cheeks had turned rosy. "And guess what, Miles? You're in luck. Davy will need a middle name."

He stretched his legs out in front of him. "I was just kidding."

"Well, I'm not. David Miles LeClaire. I like the sound of it, don't you?"

He liked the sound of it way too much. "You sure?" The two words came out rough and low.

Her glowing smile got wider. "It's a done deal. Get used to it."

Should he argue that he hadn't done all that much, certainly not enough to be her baby boy's middle-namesake?

Forget that. She wouldn't have offered if she hadn't meant it. "I, uh, thanks. I'm honored."

For several very enjoyable seconds, they just sat there, grinning at each other.

Then she picked up her iPhone. "I should…"

"Make your calls." He rose. "I'll go get your things from the car."

Miles took his time with the short errand. He sat in the waiting area for a while drinking vending-machine coffee, giving Josie privacy while she shared her big news with her family.

When he returned to the room, Davy was back in his bassinet and Josie had finished her calls. She said that both of her sisters and her aunt would be heading for the farm right away.

And then she eyed the suitcase and diaper bag. "Thanks for bringing those—did you say you brought along the car seat, too?"

"It's in the pickup. No sense in dragging it in here. I would just have to carry it out again when you're ready to home."

"Miles," she chided. "Really. It's too much. You don't have to—"

"Hey. I'm taking you home. That's what neighbors are for." His reluctance to leave kind of surprised him. He considered himself a helpful guy. But, as a rule, if someone said they could manage on their own, he left them to it.

She asked, "You're sure?"

"Positive. And if they're going to feed you before we go, I wouldn't mind a little something myself."

"You got it."

"And what about the morning chores at Wild Rose? Let me call Rafe. He'll get going on them."

"No way," she said. "You've done too much already. I gave the Huckstons a call just now. They're heading right over to Wild Rose to take care of everything." A father-son team, Tom and Kyle Huckston owned a small farm on the other side of Josie's. Their bees produced excellent honey.

A little while later, over meat loaf and mashed potatoes, Miles apologized for not bringing her straight to the hospital when she asked him to. "I might've had a little flashback there."

She nodded slowly. "Hazel mentioned once that you were in the army after nine-eleven."

He snorted out a laugh. "I was in the army, yeah. But I didn't mean a flashback from my time in the Middle East. I meant that the last thing I ever want to do is deliver another baby on the side of the road."

Josie laughed, too. "Right. You said Ashley was born on the way to the hospital..."

"Yes, she was. I was a basket case, scared out of my wits through the whole thing. Take my advice and never have a baby in the cab of a pickup."

"You've convinced me. I won't do that."

"Good. Though in the end, it did work out. Ashley was fine, and so was Fiona." As he said his wife's name, he tried not to dread what Josie would probably say next. Even three years after her death, people still felt compelled to offer him condolences. They meant only to comfort him, but their sympathy just reminded him of all the lies he tried not to think about.

Josie didn't go there. Probably because she and her family had been to the funeral. They'd offered their sympathies then. She said softly, "So it worked out when Ashley was born and it worked out for Davy, too. I think you're the guy to count on in a precipitous birth." She said it teasingly, and he appreciated her keeping it light.

He thought how pretty she was, even wearing a wrinkled floral-patterned hospital gown with dark circles under her eyes. He liked her hair, full and springy in those long corkscrew curls, pulled back now into a loose ponytail. And that smile of hers could really light up a man's day.

Funny how life went. Though Josie had grown up next door to him, he'd never spent much time with her. He'd never given her much thought beyond an honest appreciation of her as a good person, a fine farmer and a skilled veterinarian. In all the years he'd known her, it had never occurred to him that he might enjoy hanging out with her.

It was occurring to him now, though.

He remembered the ambulance issue. "I did kind of wonder if you'll be stuck with the cost of an ambulance ride..."

"Miles." She pinched up that lush mouth at him. "Stop it."

"What?"

"You're not responsible for the ambulance ride, and besides, my insurance will cover it."

He ate a spoonful of bland mashed potatoes. "That's all I needed to know."

She pointed her fork at him. "You could have just asked."

"I was working up to it—and don't give me that disapproving look. I'm just being a good neighbor and looking after the mother of my middle-namesake."

She slid her paper napkin in beside her plate and pushed away the bed tray. "You better watch out. I'll take total advantage of you."

"I doubt that—but if you do, it's okay. I like to help out. Makes me feel useful."

It was past one that afternoon when Miles stopped his crew cab behind a fancy hybrid SUV in front of Josie's little house at Wild Rose Farm.

Josie's older sister, Alexandra, a corporate law-yer who lived in Portland, emerged from the house as Miles got out to help carry the suitcase and baby gear inside.

"You're here!" Josie cried, and ran to her big sister's open arms.

Alex took Josie's face between her hands. "God. You're a mother. And you know what? Motherhood looks good on you."

Josie gave Alex a warm, happy smile. "Motherhood looks exhausting on me." She grabbed her sister's hand. "Come on. I need you to meet Davy…"

Miles waited by the driver's door as the two of them cooed over the baby. Josie unhooked the car seat and pulled it out with Davy still in it, all wrapped up against the cold in a fleece onesie, warm blanket and knit cap.

Alex grinned at Miles across the roof of his truck. "I hear you saved the day and delivered my nephew safe and sound."

He'd always liked Alex. She was tough and supersmart. Nothing got by her. "Your sister did all the work."

"But you were right there on the case when she needed you," said Alex. "You got her through it. Thank you, Miles."

He cast a glance at Josie.

"Okay," she said. "I confess. When I called my sisters and my aunt to tell them about Davy, I just had to share how you came to my rescue."

He felt a little flustered at the dewy look on her face. "Just being a good neighbor." He opened the back-seat door on his side to grab the suitcase and the diaper bag.

They all went into the house, a simple one-story cottage, the front door opening directly into the living room.

Josie instructed him, "Just leave that stuff right here. Want some coffee? I've got cupcakes, too. Chocolate with cream-cheese frosting. I baked them yesterday during a wild spurt of nesting behavior."

He wanted to stay. But her sister was here to look after her and Davy until their other sister and their aunt Marilyn arrived. Josie and Alex would want to catch up. "Nah, I should get moving. I'll bring Tink over in a few."

Josie nuzzled her newborn son's cheek. "I'll say it again." She sent Miles a glance that bordered on intimate, a glance that spoke of all they'd been through together since the dark hours of early that morning, and he felt warm all over. "Thank you. So much." Behind her, Alex looked on, a speculative gleam in her eyes. Josie's sister was too sharp by half.

Well, so what? Nothing to see here. "That's what neighbors are for," he said gruffly. "Back soon."

He got out of there fast and returned with the dog ten minutes later.

As he opened the front passenger door and Tinkerbell jumped out, Josie emerged from the house with a plastic container. Tink headed straight for her. Josie held the container in one hand as she bent to pet her dog with the other. "I can see you've been a really good girl." Tink whined in happy agreement.

Rising, Josie let the dog into the cottage. Miles hesitated there by his truck.

Josie shut the cottage door and came down the steps to him. "No way I can let you go without cupcakes," she said.

"You didn't have to—"

"What?" She stopped a couple feet from him and pooched out her soft lower lip. "You don't want my cupcakes?" Even with her hair in a pony-tail, the thick mass refused to behave. The cold winter wind tugged at it, sending corkscrew curls bouncing.

He had to remind himself not to grin like a fool. "Of course, I want your cupcakes."

"Right answer." She poked his chest with the container, and he took it from her.

After that, there was nothing more to do but dip his chin in a nod of thanks and go home.

At Halstead Farm, Miles collected Bruce and visited the henhouse to gather any eggs they'd laid since Rafe had checked earlier. Miles used incandescent lights and infrared heat in the winter to keep the hens laying, but the eggs could still freeze if not gathered promptly.

Once he'd dry-cleaned the eggs and stored them in the fridge in the garage, he went inside and took a shower. By then, he was hungry. He ate leftovers, after which he remembered that he hadn't brought Josie's cupcakes in from the truck.

He went and got them, eating one on the spot out there in the garage and then gobbling up another once he got back to the kitchen. They were delicious. He had to restrain himself from wolfing down every last one of those suckers on the spot.

As he firmly put the lid back on the container, he wondered how Josie and Davy were doing... and then put a lid on that thought, as well.

Josie was feeling the love.

Payton, with her husband, Easton, and their twin boys, arrived from Seattle in time for dinner. Auntie M and her boyfriend, Ernesto, were still on their way up from Salinas, where Ernesto owned an artichoke farm.

Payton, Easton and the four-year-old boys, Penn and Bailey, all wanted to hold the baby. Alex whipped out her phone and snapped pictures of the twins sitting on the sofa cradling Davy, who was all wrapped up like a burrito, between them.

"He's so beautiful," Payton said with a sigh as she scooped up Davy and put him on her shoulder. She and Easton shared one of their hot looks. They wanted another baby. Payton had confided in Josie that they'd stopped using birth control.

Before dawn the next morning, Auntie M and Ernesto arrived. Josie just happened to be up nursing Davy when she heard the crunch of Ernesto's tires as his big Ram 3500 rolled past her house on the way to Aunt Marilyn's.

Auntie M must have seen the light on. A few minutes later, she tapped on the front door. Josie, carrying Davy, went to answer, with Tink at her heels.

"Oh, sweetheart." Auntie M took off her heavy Pendleton jacket and hooked it on one of the wall pegs by the door. Look at you…" She gathered them both into her long, slim arms. Josie breathed in the much-loved scent of her lilac perfume. "I wasn't going to wake you."

"But you saw the light in the front bedroom, I know. And I'm glad you did."

"I simply could not resist." She took Josie by the arms and held her away. "I only need to get my hands on him—just for a minute or two."

Josie gave her the bundled baby. Auntie M cradled him, cooing to him as she gently swayed from side to side. She looked up, tears shining in her green eyes. "I'm sorry I wasn't here."

"Don't be. It all went fine, I promise you. I mean, as fine as pushing out a baby ever can be."

They went and sat at the kitchen table, Tink stretching out beside Josie's chair, Auntie M still holding the sleeping Davy. "Is he nursing all right?"

"Like a champ. My milk's not in yet, but Davy's no quitter."

Davy yawned hugely. Auntie M said, "I'm so glad Miles was home."

"Me, too." Josie felt a warm flush of gratitude toward Miles—and something else, too. Something tender and fond. He really had taken such good care of her and Davy when it mattered the most. "You want coffee? I'll make some."

Auntie M shook her head. "You need to sleep while this little angel is sleeping. Here." She handed Davy back. Josie took the warm bundle eagerly. He'd been born only yesterday and already she couldn't imagine her life without him.

She trailed after her aunt to the door.

"Breakfast at my house," Auntie M said. "French-toast casserole."

It was a family tradition, that casserole. Josie's mouth watered just thinking about it. "We'll be there, me and Davy, with bells on."

Her aunt put on her jacket and then knelt to give Tink a scratch behind her pointy ears. "Seven or so?"

"See you then."

After one last hug, Auntie M went out the door.

Payton and her brood joined them for breakfast at Marilyn's house. Alex, too. She'd spent last night in Auntie M's guest room and would be leaving for Portland after dinner tonight. Alex worked long hours at the law firm of Kauffman, Judd and Tisdale. She rarely stayed at the farm for more than a day or two at a stretch.

Josie scarfed down her aunt's French toast and basked in family togetherness. It was like old times—only better, with Davy there.

Gratitude…

Yes. She felt it so strongly now. Gratitude for her healthy newborn son and for her family, all of whom came running when she needed them.

Feeling thankful had her thinking of Miles again. He was seven or eight years older, so Josie hadn't gone to school with him or anything. They'd simply known each other all their lives, just without really *knowing* each other.

She felt so much closer to him now. She felt she could honestly call him a friend—and as a friend, she found herself thinking about Miles, the man, more deeply.

Josie hadn't even reached her teens when Miles joined the army. He came back a few years later, started working on the farm. She'd heard that he was taking classes at Portland State and also that he'd met Fiona in Portland. They'd married. After that, he'd always seemed happy—with his life as a farmer, with Fiona, whom he'd clearly adored, and with their daughters.

The loss of his true love had hit the guy hard, though, and understandably so. Since Fiona's death a mile from home during her morning jog, of cardiac arrest from undiagnosed hypertrophic cardiomyopathy, Miles had changed. Even to a casual acquaintance like Josie, the difference in him was noticeable. He'd grown quieter; he kept to himself more.

But, boy, did he step right up for Josie and Davy when it mattered. She would need to find a way to repay him for his kindness, for being a stand-up guy in the truest sense of the word. Cupcakes weren't near enough. At least he'd seemed pleased that she'd given Davy his middle name...

"What are you grinning about?" Alex eyed her across the breakfast table.

Josie gave an easy shrug. "Just happy you're all here."

"Ri-i-i-ight..." Alex drew out the word, almost like she knew exactly what Josie had been thinking.

News traveled pretty fast in the Heartwood community.

When Ashley and Hazel arrived home from

their grandmother's on Sunday afternoon, they already knew that Josie had had her baby at their house, and that their dad had helped with the birth.

Thirteen-year-old Hazel burst into the house chattering excitedly about how Darlene the nurse had told her daughter about the baby and Aurora had turned right around and called her best friend, Ashley. "And Ashley told me and Grandma. Rory's mom said both Josie and the baby are doing great."

"Yes, they are," he replied. "I drove them home from the hospital yesterday. Alex was waiting on Josie's front step to take care of them."

Hazel idolized Josie and wanted to be a veterinarian just like her when she grew up. "I'm so glad you were here to help." Dropping her overnight bag, she threw her arms around his waist.

He gave her a squeeze. "Me, too."

"You're the best, Dad," she announced. Scooping up her bag again, she ran upstairs to her room. Five minutes later, she came racing back down. "Dad. May I *please* just go on over to Wild Rose for a little while. I can't wait to see that baby…"

"She's got the family visiting, Haze—her aunt and Payton should also be there by now. Maybe you ought to wait a few days."

"*Ple-e-ease*, Dad. I won't stay long. I won't be annoying. I promise I won't. I want to see the twins…and the kittens, too." Hazel used to babysit Payton's two boys. And she still loved helping Josie with the various animals she rescued, including a pregnant stray cat that had given birth just the week before.

How was he supposed to resist those pleading eyes? "Be back in an hour," he said gruffly.

That got him a giant smile. "Thanks." Hazel flew out the door.

As for his older daughter, Ashley's current priorities overrode meeting Josie's new baby and petting a stray cat's litter of kittens. Sixteen and as pretty as her mother had been, with thick dark hair and hazel eyes, Ashley was all about her social life with her school friends. While Hazel had paused to greet him and give him a hug, Ashley had gone straight up to her room. Ten minutes later, she came back down to announce that she *had* to return to town. "We've got that history project, Dad. Rory and I need to work on it."

"You had the whole weekend to work on your project with Aurora."

She gave him a heavy sigh paired with an eye roll. "What can I tell you? It's not done, and we have to finish it."

Miles did realize that Ashley needed a certain amount of independence. "All right."

"Thanks, Dad."

"Drive carefully. Be home at five thirty for dinner."

"*Five thirty?* Dad, come on. It's almost three. I can eat at Rory's—Rory's mom invited me. And I'll be home by ten."

"You've been gone all weekend. Five thirty. Yes or no?"

"Nine?" she pleaded. When he shook his head, she offered, "Eight?"

He finally gave a little. "Six thirty. Take it or leave it."

Five minutes later, she drove off in the trusty secondhand VW Golf he'd bought her for her sixteenth birthday.

Hazel, pink-cheeked and smiling, returned forty-five minutes after Ashley left. She told Miles all about how she got to hold Davy and she just knew he'd smiled at her, even though Payton said that babies didn't know how to smile on purpose until they were a couple months old.

Eyes shining, she beamed up at him. "I also got to visit the kittens—Dad, they're adorable. One's a calico and she's the cutest thing ever. Josie said she will be giving them away to good homes and baby calico can be mine—Dad, she's so sweet. You will love her so much. She'll be spayed and up-to-date on shots by the time I get her. Josie has an arrangement with the shelter in town and they come to the farm and get the kittens, treat them at Heartwood Animal Clinic and then bring them back. And then, when we adopt, we pay for everything, but at a very low price. So it's a deal we'll be getting, I promise you that."

He gave her a patient look and said gently, "I don't think so, honey."

Hazel said nothing for several seconds. She amazed him sometimes. Only thirteen, yet she read him so well. Finally, she suggested, "How about this, Dad? Maybe we can talk about it later?"

"Maybe."

"And one more thing." Wasn't there always? "Josie's going to need a little help with the kittens. She didn't ask, but after her family leaves, I want to offer to go over there at least once a day. I could clean the litter box, change the water and put down food for the mama. The kittens will need socializing. And in a few weeks, they should start litter-box training…"

"What? Kittens need training to use a litter box, now?"

"Well, most of them don't. They pick it up naturally by watching the mama cat. But some do need a little help." Hazel gazed up at him, so sweet and hopeful. "What do you think?"

"I think you're a good neighbor. And yeah, talk to Josie. If she agrees, that's fine with me."

Hazel hugged him and headed for her room to unpack her suitcase. He thought how he would probably end up agreeing to take on that kitten she wanted, and not just because he had trouble saying no to his girls.

Miles had zero doubt that Hazel would not only agree to scoop litter and make sure the cat had food and water, but she would also actually do the chores she'd promised to do. With Hazel, he cherished the hope that she might make it through her teen years without once slamming her bedroom door—okay, maybe that was unrealistic. But what did a man have if he didn't have hope?

Hazel helped him get dinner on the table and pitched in cleaning up afterward.

Ashley breezed back in at seven thirty. Miles tried to talk to her about keeping her agreements. That didn't go well. She stomped off to her room in a huff.

The sound of her door slamming had barely stopped reverberating through the house when his mother, Donna, called.

"Word is out, son," she said. "You're a local hero now."

He laughed and downplayed his part in Davy's birth. But he did feel good about it, glad that he'd been there, that he'd been able to help.

Too bad Davy's birth wasn't all she'd called to talk about. "I think we also need to talk a little about Ashley," she began. "Miles, I hate to be a snitch, but Ashley spent most of the weekend with her friends. Hazel and I hardly saw her..."

He tried placating. "Sorry, Mom. I'll talk to her."

His mother let out a hard huff of breath. "Miles, be realistic. Talking doesn't work with her. You've got to set boundaries and then make her stick to them."

He rubbed at his temple, where a headache threatened, and reminded himself of how grateful he was that his mom took an active role as a grandmother. Fiona's parents weren't even in the picture. They had divorced when Fiona was young, and each had remarried. Fiona had always said that she'd never felt close to them. They sent cards and gifts, but never came to visit or invited the girls to come to them.

"Miles," said his mother impatiently. "Are you still there?"

"Right here, Mom." And he just couldn't keep his damn mouth shut. He began defending Ashley. "You know she's a good kid. Some kids you can't discipline into submission."

"Miles Stanley Halstead, that girl has your number."

It went on like that. Miles alternately defended his daughter and tried to pacify his mother, who repeatedly informed him that he was going about raising Ashley all wrong.

When she finally let him off the phone, he had to take two ibuprofens to get rid of his headache.

Miles grabbed the remote and tried to watch a Blazers game. But his mind kept wandering back to the birth of his neighbor's son. He'd loved being helpful and more or less indispensable, not to mention feeling like a million bucks with all the thanks and praise Josie had heaped on him.

No doubt about it. Helping to deliver a baby was so much easier than fighting with his daughter and then having to listen to his mother lecture him about how he needed to be tougher on Ashley, lay down the law with her, draw the line on her more, the way Fiona used to do. And, yeah, despite the betrayals and lies he'd only found about after she died, Fiona had been a good mother overall—she'd been gone more than was ideal, but firm and clear with her daughters about what was expected of them. Miles had to give his deceased wife credit for that. And *his* mother ought to understand that he and his girls were doing the best that they could.

Both of his daughters had suffered when they lost Fiona. But Hazel had always been more of a daddy's girl. She'd clung to Miles for comfort, as he had to her. Ashley, though, had outright adored her mother. His older daughter loved that her mom was beautiful, stylish and sophisticated. Ashley had looked up to Fiona in all things. When Fiona died, Ashley lost her guiding force, her north star.

And Ashley damn well deserved a little leeway now. She needed the space to find her own way.

Miles reached down to pet Bruce and smiled to himself as an image of Josie drifted into his mind. He could see her in his mind's eye, crouched on his porch in the darkest part of Saturday morning, groaning, those amber eyes anxious in her flushed face.

How was she doing today?

Maybe he ought to check on her, see if she needed anything.

"Uh-uh," he said under his breath.

He would only be butting in, looking to be helpful when she already had her people around her.

Josie had her family with her now, ready to take care of the day-to-day stuff. Her family would cook the meals, help with Davy, manage everything at the farm.

Later, though. After they all went back to their own lives.

He would be there to help out if she needed him then.

Chapter Three

At Wild Rose Farm, Alex stayed on until ten that night. But then she said she had to get back. She needed to be at work first thing Monday morning. Josie hated to see her go.

Still, she had nothing to complain about. Auntie M, Ernesto, and Payton and her brood did stay. Auntie M and Payton got right on the job of finding Josie a dependable year-round farmhand.

They put the word out that Wild Rose Farm needed an experienced hand. By midweek, they'd hired a dependable local man. Clark Stockwell arrived with his own double-wide trailer to live in.

He also brought two horses and a sweet-natured black Labrador retriever named Big Nose.

A gentle, quiet fellow, born and raised in Heartwood, Clark knew farm work. Josie felt confident in trusting him to take care of the animals, tend the winter garden and prune the pear and apple trees. With Clark to help out, she would have no problem running Wild Rose.

Easton went home next. He left for Seattle on Saturday. Payton's husband needed to get back to work as CEO of his family's hotel business, Wright Hospitality.

The good news, though? Payton and her boys stayed for another week. But then they were gone—and the next day, Auntie M and Ernesto packed up the big red pickup and headed for Salinas.

Josie promised herself she wouldn't cry when they left. She had an excellent farmhand now. She could manage at the farm on her own. Payton and Aunt Marilyn returned often, and they always came through when she needed them. They did not have to live a short walk from Josie's front door.

Still, after watching her aunt drive away with Ernesto, she went back in her house, checked on her sweetly sleeping baby, carefully shut the bedroom door...and burst into tears. Not because she had it so rough.

But because she missed Payton. She yearned for her nephews. Auntie M had only just left, but Josie felt her aunt's absence like she had a hole in her heart and a cold wind was blowing through it, freezing her from the inside out.

She loved her son. So much. Davy was everything.

But it wasn't supposed to be like this. It wasn't supposed to be just her and Davy, alone.

Yes, she wanted her sister and her aunt to follow their own dreams, to live their best life with the men they loved, but that didn't stop her from feeling miserable and sorry for herself in private.

As she cried into a soggy wad of tissues, trying to keep her sobs quiet in order not to wake the baby, something nudged her knee.

Tink had come to comfort her. With a whine of love and understanding, the sweet girl plunked her head on Josie's lap. Josie curved over her and snuggled into the warm, coarse fur at her neck. "Don't worry, honey," she whispered. "I'm on this. I'm going to pull myself together any minute now."

Tink whined again and nuzzled Josie's cheek. For a few minutes, Josie basked in the love of her dog and the luxurious self-indulgence of a full-out, ugly cry.

But then came the sudden wail from the front bedroom.

"Shh," she whispered to the dog, though she herself was the one making all the noise. "Maybe he'll just go back to sleep…"

But he didn't.

Josie dried her eyes and went to get him.

Tuesday after school, Hazel tracked down Miles in the horse barn and asked for permission to visit Wild Rose Farm. "I not only need to see about the kittens, I want to visit Josie and see baby Davy."

He gave his permission, reminding her to say hi to Josie for him and give the baby a hug. Hazel promised to do both.

At dinner that night, she reported that *her* kitten, the *adorable* calico, had nine weeks to go before she would be ready to leave her mom and move in with her forever family.

Miles tried not to smile. "*Your* kitten, huh?" He buttered a dinner roll.

"It's good to think positive, Dad. Positivity matters." Across the table, Ashley rolled her eyes. Hazel called her on it. "I saw that, Ash. What? You don't believe in positivity?"

Ashley gave a cool little half shrug. "Not really. Sometimes you can be super positive about something and still not get what you want. Believe me, I ought to know." Ashley added a hair toss, just to drive her point home.

Miles asked, "What didn't you get that you wanted, Ashley?"

Her sigh was long and very bored. "Dad. I was just, you know, speaking theoretically."

"Are you sure? Sounded to me like you were talking about something that had happened to you."

Fiona's eyes stared at him out of their daughter's pretty, pouty face. "I'm fine, Dad. I only meant that people think they can wish something into happening and they can't, that's all."

"Well, if you could wish for something, what would it be?"

Ashley blew out both cheeks and showed him the hand. "Stop." He didn't know whether to laugh or groan in frustration. Why did he never get it right with Ash? Before he could decide what to say next, she announced, "I'm finished eating. May I be excused? I really need to call Rory."

"Right now?"

"A short call, Dad, then I'll come back and help with the dishes."

"Fifteen minutes."

"Promise." She even forced a smile.

Miles let her go. His attempts to start meaningful conversations with his older daughter rarely went anywhere and just now was only more of the same.

He turned to Hazel. "So how are Josie and the baby doing?"

"They're fine. Davy's so sweet. I got to hold him. I love his hands, so tiny and perfect. And his little bitty mouth." She ate another bite of the stew he'd had slow-cooking all day. "Josie says I'll get to babysit him soon." She drank some milk, then carefully set down the glass. "And she said she would love it if I would check in on the kittens once or twice a day to help take care of them, so we're set with that."

"You're kind to do it, Hazel."

Her cheeks pinkened. "Well, I love to take care of animals."

"I know you do."

"Josie does seem a little…"

Miles leaned in. "A little what?"

Hazel shook herself. "I think she misses her family, you know?"

Did ears actually perk up? He felt that his just had. "Are they gone, then, her sisters and Marilyn?"

"Mmm-hmm. They all left. Now it's just Josie and Davy and the new guy they hired."

"A new guy?" He meant to sound merely curious, but it might have come out a little more aggressive than he'd intended.

"Yeah."

Miles had no doubt that Josie needed someone dependable to help out. He just hoped they hadn't hired her some drifter. His stomach knotted at the thought. "A new farmhand?"

Hazel gave him one of her patient looks, a look that said, *I love you, Dad. But you need to put on your listening ears.* "Yeah, Dad. A new guy, like I said."

"Did you get his name?"

She frowned. "Um, Clark something, I think…"

"Stockwell?"

"That's it. Clark Stockwell."

Miles breathed easier. "Clark's a good man." Stockwell had worked for the Huckstons for years but then moved to Bend. Apparently, the move hadn't worked out.

Hazel ate more stew. "Josie said he's great, that they were lucky to get him."

"Good, good. So you think Josie is managing okay, then?"

"Sure. Of course…"

Miles was leaning in again. "You sound doubtful."

"Well, she does seem a little sad, you know?"

"How so?"

"Just quieter, I guess. I asked her if she was okay."

"And?"

"She admitted that she misses her family, but then she got all cheerful and said she was only being self-indulgent, that I shouldn't listen to her, that everything was going just great."

After breakfast on Wednesday morning, Josie fed and changed Davy, and bundled him up nice and warm. He fussed a little when she put him back down in his bassinet in order to pile on her own outdoor gear.

For the first time, she hooked him, nice and cozy, to the front of her in his new baby sling. She'd read up on slings and even gotten a few lessons in how to use them at the birthing class she'd taken.

Several websites claimed it was possible to put a newborn in a back sling, but that would take more skill than she currently possessed, and maybe a helper to get him positioned correctly.

Well, she had no helper, and her baby couldn't hold up his head. He could have trouble breathing if she hooked him back there wrong. Having him on the front of her put more limitations on what chores she could tackle. But for now, it was the best she could do.

And she was sick of being cooped up in the house. She needed to get out, do something constructive beyond housework and taking care of her baby.

Davy seemed to like the sling. He stopped fussing and settled right in, close to her body heat and the sound of her heartbeat. She put on warm gloves and her wool hat. Clicking her tongue for Tink, who got up and fell in behind her, she went out into the cold, overcast morning.

She found Clark tinkering with the older of the farm's two John Deere utility tractors in the large shed they used to store and maintain equipment. His aging Lab, Big Nose, was lying curled up close by.

"Miz LeClaire!" Clark looked mildly startled at the sight of her.

"It's Josie," she corrected, and not for the first time. Clark was in his late forties at most. It just seemed so odd for a man that age to be calling her "Miz."

"Right. Josie." He grabbed a greasy rag to wipe his hands as Big Nose lurched to his feet and wriggled over to greet her. Josie gave him a quick pat on the head, and he moved on to Tink. The dogs sniffed at each other in a friendly way, tails wagging. Meanwhile, Clark eyed the bulge of her baby beneath the baby sling. "Everything okay?"

"I thought maybe you could use a little help."

"You sure?"

She laughed, which felt kind of good, really, and lightly stroked the curve of Davy's back through the sling. "I'll just check on the kittens in the rescue barn, see how they're doing."

There were four barns on Wild Rose, built over

the years for various purposes. Josie and Payton had fixed up one of them for events, including Payton and Easton's wedding last New Year's Day. Josie used another, which she'd dubbed the rescue barn, to care for orphaned, ill, stray or abused animals she looked after until she found them good homes. Currently, the mama cat and her litter of five were the only ones staying there.

"I looked in on them already this morning, checked on the water and food situations," Clark reported. "The Halstead girl told me she'll be helping to take care of them. Yesterday, I added that second litter box like you said."

"Thank you. I know you've been making sure they have everything they need, and I wasn't really planning to scoop litter or feed them. I just need my kitten fix."

Clark gave her his slow, careful smile. "I get that. Those kittens are cute."

"I can't wait to visit them. And after that, I'll do what I can in the greenhouse, get some of the herbs started. I probably won't last long, but I really wanted to get out of the house."

"Uh, sure Miz—Josie. Just give a holler if you need anything."

"Thanks, Clark. I will."

With a nod, he turned back to the old tractor.

It was a short walk to the rescue barn. Inside,

she told Tink to lie down, and the dog stretched out by the door.

"Good girl." Josie went on through an inner door to what used to be a tack room and found mama cat stretched out on a bed of hay, her babies crawling all over her and each other. They all seemed healthy and content. The babies were walking now, hardly wobbling at all. For half an hour, Josie hung out with them.

Next, in the greenhouse with its smelly pile of compost in the center and bubble-wrapped walls to keep the heat in, she turned on the propane heater and the fans, switched her winter gloves for nitrile gardening gloves and started seeds for celery, oregano, rosemary and thyme. For an hour, she hummed to herself and poked seeds in black dirt. With her baby warm against her heart and her dog at her feet, she felt at peace with the world.

But then Davy began squirming. He was full-out wailing by the time she gave up and turned off the heater and the fans. Over her baby's angry cries, she let Clark know she was heading back to the house. The farmhand looked nothing short of relieved to see her go.

With a wave, she headed for the cottage. Once inside, she set to work untangling her baby from the sling. Davy screamed even louder through that, but she did manage, finally, to get him out of the sling. She had to put him down on the bed for a minute to shed her outerwear. He screamed even louder.

At least the silence when he latched on and started nursing was pure heaven.

After the regular routine of feeding and changing, he went back to sleep. She let Tink out for a while and cleaned up the kitchen, then made her own bed, as quietly as possible, because Davy slept in the bassinet right next to it. After that, in beautiful silence for over an hour, sitting at her small corner desk in the living area, she worked on her tax returns.

She was headed to the front door to call Tink back inside when the doorbell rang. Wincing at the sound, she yanked the door wide and found Tink—and Miles Halstead—waiting on the other side.

Tink bumped in around her.

Miles, who looked wonderfully big and broad and solid in a down jacket, worn jeans and heavy work boots, asked warily, "What? Everything okay?"

She put a finger to her lips. They stared at each other as she waited for the sound of her baby's fussy cries.

He mouthed, *Davy?*

She nodded, and then breathed a sigh of gratitude for small favors when she heard only silence from the other room. "Come on in. Coffee?"

"Now you're talking." He gave her that great smile of his, kind of shy and a little reluctant. It was a smile that made her feel special for causing it.

She brewed a fresh pot, poured hot water over a teabag for herself and put a plate of applesauce muffins on the table between them. As she filled his mug, she heard the first tentative whines from her bedroom.

He sipped his coffee. "We could take odds on whether or not he'll go back to sleep."

"As long as I get to bet that he won't," she muttered in reply as she sat down. The cries increased in volume. After that went on for a bit, she flashed Miles a forced smile. "I'll be right back."

"I'll be here."

Her throat clutched a little, that he wasn't already halfway to the door. *Props to you, Miles Halstead. You're braver than most guys.*

Five minutes later, with a soft cotton scarf draped over her bare breast and her nursing baby, she was settled in the chair across from Miles again. "So what's up?"

He ate the last of a muffin. "Just checking on my middle-namesake and his mother. I heard your sister and aunt left."

"Yeah." Her throat tightened again, this time with a spurt of self-pity. She swallowed it down. It pissed her off that all her emotions lurked so close to the surface lately. "But everything's fine, really. I have good help—including Hazel, by the way. She's an angel to volunteer to look after the kittens and their mama."

"She's thrilled to do it."

"Well, I really appreciate it. Did she tell you we hired Clark Stockwell?"

"She did."

"So we're in great shape."

He rested one long arm on the table. She stared at his big, lean, capable hand as he said, "Looks like the little guy's doing well."

"Yes, he is." She said it cheerfully, but maybe it came out sounding a bit brittle.

There was silence from the other side of the table. Slowly, she raised her gaze to meet his and he asked, "So how come you look like you're about to start screaming as loud as that baby was a few minutes ago?"

She straightened her shoulders. "I am not about to start screaming." He gazed back at her so patiently, and she felt the hot burn of tears all over again. With a grunt of sheer irritation at herself for not being tougher, she confessed, "All right. I'm feeling sorry for myself and hating myself for it. I miss my family, okay? Satisfied now?"

"Did you tell them that? Did you ask them not to leave yet?"

"Of course not." To escape the kindness in his

pale blue eyes, she readjusted the scarf that covered the baby. "You're just waiting for me to explain myself further, aren't you?" she accused without looking up at him again. "Well, okay then. I'll tell you. If I asked them, they would stay."

"Then ask them and they'll come back."

"No. The point is, my life is here, on Wild Rose Farm. My aunt's life and Payton's life are elsewhere now. So is Alex's life, for that matter—hers always has been. But they do look after me. They help out. They do their share to make things work here. Payton and Easton are paying Clark's salary. Anything I need, I only have to ask for it and they make sure it happens. They all still love the farm. Payton will be showing up for weeks in the summer. It's only February and they're already talking about coming here for the holidays, all of them, Easton's parents included. It's not like I'll never see them. It's only that I'm having trouble accepting that my sisters and my aunt just don't live here anymore. We had…"

She paused, searching for the right words. "Our family ways, you know—my aunt and Payton and me. Every Sunday we would have breakfast together at Auntie M's. And when it was Payton's morning for chores, she would call me and I would go over to her house in my pajamas and doze on the couch, keeping an eye on the twins while she gathered eggs and fed the animals. It's just, the rhythms of a day, I guess. Having your people right there to talk to whenever you need them..."

He was so quiet. She slanted him a glance and found him watching her—not judging, more like kind of taking it all in.

And she realized she felt better, much better. Simply to be sitting here across from him, having him look at her like whatever crazy postpartum hormones she needed to exercise right now, he could take it. He was here for her.

She gave him a wobbly little smile. "I put Davy in a sling and worked for an hour in the greenhouse today," she added, softly now, feeling happy to have someone just sitting there. And listening. "It was good. Really good."

Right then, under the scarf, Davy popped off her breast and made a grumpy little sound.

She and Miles shared a grin as she eased her son out from under the makeshift cover. "I've got a burp cloth around here somewhere." Miles grabbed it from the chair next to him and passed it over to her. "Thank you."

He poured himself a second cup of coffee. She burped the baby and then put him to her other breast.

"Your daughter wants a kitten," she said, once Davy was comfortably settled.

Miles laughed, a deep, attractive sound, unassuming and genuine. "I know. She's counting the days until *her* kitten is old enough to come and live with us."

"Aha. So you've said yes to adopting one?"

He pretended to glower. "I haven't said yes or no yet."

"But you will say yes, won't you?"

"I'm not answering that."

Josie leaned in. "I won't say a word to her. Your secret is safe with me."

They talked about Hazel for a while. And then about how his mom was doing, living on her own in town.

When Davy finished eating, Miles asked to hold him.

"Sure." Rising, she circled the table and laid him in Miles's arms.

Waving his little fists, Davy made nonsense sounds and stared up at the big guy who cradled him. When Davy scrunched up his face and his cheeks turned red, Miles said, "Looks like there's a diaper change in your future, David Miles."

Laughing, her heart lighter now than it had been since she'd watched Auntie M and Ernesto drive away, she got up again. Miles handed Davy over. She took him to the sofa and changed him on the pad from his diaper bag.

Miles came and stood above her, his hands in his pockets. "Do you have a changing table?"

She gave him a quick smile, then focused on the

baby again. "Yeah, in the back bedroom, which will be his room. So far, I don't go in there much. True confession, it's not really finished yet. I need to put in some shelves, get everything organized. I did a wall mural for him right after Christmas, but never got around to painting the rest of the room. It's no rush. I'll keep him in the bassinet in my room for the next couple of months, anyway."

Pulling one hand from his pocket, Miles scraped back the chestnut hair that had flopped over his forehead. "Can I have a look?"

She eased Davy's feet back into his fleece onesie and snapped it up. "The mural is cute. It's from a stencil kit I bought online, but I confess I'm a slacker. I've let getting the room together slide. Then when Payton and Auntie M offered to finish it for me, I turned them down."

His steady gaze stayed right on her. "Why?"

"I don't know. I was thinking I should have no problem finishing it myself long before he needs it. I spend most of my time right here in the house, and half of that time, he's sleeping. So I *will* get to it. As of now, though, all his stuff is just stacked in there, waiting for me to pull it together."

He tipped his head to the side in a thoughtful way and said quietly, "You should let people help you."

"I do. And they do help me. A lot. *You've* helped me...and okay, yeah. When Payton and

Auntie M offered, I should've just told them to go for it. But I didn't. Like I said, I'll get to it eventually. It's really no problem."

For that, she got a shrug of one broad shoulder, followed by a question. "So can I have a look?"

"Not much to see…"

Miles simply gazed at her, waiting.

"Fine." She took Davy in her arms and led the way to the back bedroom. "Ta-da!"

He stepped around the baby furniture shoved together in the middle of the room and stood with his back to her, facing the mural. "A farm scene, huh?"

"Super imaginative, right?"

He turned to her. "Nothing wrong with a good farm scene—where are you thinking of mounting the shelves?"

She pointed. "In that space beside the window. I thought I would put the bureau, with a pad on top for a changing table, under the shelves. That way I have everything right there in easy reach, you know?"

"Might be simpler to paint the wall first, before you add the shelves."

"That's the plan."

He cast a glance at the pile of things in the center of the room. "Where are the shelves?"

"I haven't decided yet whether to make them or buy them," she admitted. "I'm picturing floating shelves of natural wood, something with a nice grain and color." Davy burped in her ear. She chuckled and kissed his cheek. "I already have the paint for the walls." She pointed at the paint cans stacked in the corner and felt kind of silly trying so hard to convince him that she had everything under control. "Honestly. I *will* get to dealing with all of this eventually..."

"You said that."

"Right," she replied. "I guess I did." She breathed in her son's sweet baby scent and realized she felt almost sane again...thanks to Miles Halstead. His kindness and understanding heartened her.

Twice now, she'd told him way more about herself and her issues than he could have possibly wanted to hear. First, while giving birth to Davy, and then today. Both times he'd been amazing about it, taking it all in, giving her his attention and his unspoken permission to open up to him. At no point had she felt judged or found lacking. Instead, she'd felt supported and thoroughly understood.

"Got a tape measure handy?" he asked. "I have some gorgeous leftover western red cedar that would look great in here."

"Miles, I really can do it myself."

"Of course, you can. But there's no need for

you to do it yourself. I want to help. All you have to do is let me. You've got nothing to prove to me."

"Nothing to prove to you?" She kissed her baby's temple again and gently rocked him from side to side. "What are you getting at?"

"It seems to me that you need for your family to see you as happy and self-sufficient. You don't want them to think you need them here to get by."

It was precisely what she'd so awkwardly tried to explain to him earlier. The man surprised her at every turn. "Er, exactly?"

"But we all need a hand now and then."

"So?"

"So, Josie. Get me the tape measure."

She went and got it for him. When he left fifteen minutes later, he said he would be back with the finished shelves on Saturday.

After he drove off, she stood at the front window with Davy in her arms. "Miles is a good guy," she whispered against the silky skin of her baby's forehead.

Davy made a gurgling sound.

She kissed him again. "I'm so glad we agree." She was smiling to herself...and looking forward to Saturday.

Miles showed up as promised the following Saturday at ten in the morning accompanied by

Hazel and Bruce. He also brought a tool kit and the finished shelves.

They were absolutely gorgeous, those shelves, made of thick reclaimed cedar. Tink and Bruce stretched out in the living area and Hazel helped with the baby while Miles and Josie painted the remaining three walls of Davy's room.

They broke for lunch, which Josie provided, at a little before one. After the meal, Hazel took the dogs out to visit mama cat and the kittens in the rescue barn. The paint was dry in the baby's room by then. Miles and Josie put up the shelves.

Hazel returned in time to deal with Davy when he woke up again. Josie and Miles got to work arranging baby furniture.

Ashley arrived at four. She hugged Josie and then held the baby for a while, handing him right back to Hazel when he started to fuss. Hazel whisked him off to the front bedroom to change him, at which point Ashley started in on her dad for permission to spend the night at her friend Aurora's in town. Miles got her promise to drive carefully and be home by ten Sunday morning.

"Thanks, Dad." She pressed a kiss to his cheek and then rushed out the door.

Miles stood at the window to watch her drive away.

Josie stared at his broad back. "She gets more

beautiful every I time I see her. I'll bet all the guys are paying attention."

Miles turned and scowled at her. "Not what a sixteen-year-old girl's father ever wants to hear."

Josie folded her arms across her chest. "Face it. Your daughters are growing up."

"Go ahead. Rub it in."

She snickered. "I guess I'd better shut up or you won't help me finish setting up Davy's fabulous new room."

By five, the room was everything Josie had imagined it could be. Hazel had pitched in to help stack the beautiful new shelves with baby stuff and hang the musical mobile of dancing horses and cows over the crib.

Josie turned on the mobile. It flashed a kaleidoscope of colored lights on the ceiling and played a lullaby. They all three stood back to admire their work, Hazel between Miles and Josie, one arm around each of them.

"It looks so good," said Josie. "I can hardly believe it's all ready to go." She caught Miles's eye over Hazel's head. "Thank you." He nodded, looking pleased. Hazel glanced up at her and Josie said, "Hazel, thank *you*."

"Our work here is done," Hazel declared.

Father and daughter stayed for dinner. When they left around eight, Josie hated to see them go. And yet, she felt good, relaxed. The needy sadness that had taken hold of her after Auntie M left for Salinas had been eliminated by the kindness of the farmer next door.

She carried Davy into the nursery room and gave him a tour, shaking rattles for him, turning on the rooster lamp and the crib mobile just to impress him. No, he had no clue about any of it. He couldn't even lift up his head yet, but she pretended he loved it, anyway. She imagined him as the years went by, getting a real bed and wanting a truck theme for his room, or maybe a mural of planets and stars.

That night, for the first time, Davy slept for four hours straight.

And so did she.

Chapter Four

In the first week of March, Josie saw Miles every day. He would drop by just to check on her and Davy. Most days, he stayed for lunch. Saturday, she brought a casserole to Miles's house for dinner. Ashley ate with them, but then Miles let her go to Aurora's.

It was past ten when Josie got back to her cottage. She went to sleep that night smiling, and when Davy woke her up an hour later, she happily nursed him, changed him and sang him a lullaby until his little eyes drooped shut.

Monday, Miles showed up for lunch. It was getting to be a thing, him coming by around noon and staying for a sandwich and an hour of easy conversation. Josie was only too happy to fix him some food. That day, he held Davy while he ate. He had a way with her baby. She'd started thinking of him as her Davy whisperer.

Tuesday afternoon, Hazel had a job kid-sitting for a neighbor of her grandmother Donna's. The plan had Hazel showing up to watch the three little girls right after school got out and later spending the night at her grandmother's. Ashley saw her chance to stay the night in town, too.

Miles explained all this to Josie when he dropped by for lunch that day.

"Chicken cacciatore for dinner," Josie offered. "I mean, if you don't want to eat at home alone." Bruce, on the floor near Josie's chair, chose that moment to scratch his neck. His tags rattled. Josie leaned down to give him a pat. "Brucie, you're invited, too." The dog yawned hugely. She glanced up at Miles with a grin. "Brucie can't wait."

Miles laughed. Josie kind of loved his laugh—it was a little hesitant and yet somehow completely sincere. "Whew. I was scared there for a second or two."

"Of what?"

"That you wouldn't take the hint and I would end up at my place eating week-old leftover chili."

"Can't have my favorite dad eating just any old thing, now can I? As for that week-old chili, you should probably just throw that in the compost bin."

He shifted Davy in his big arms and gave her one of his warm steady looks. "I'll bring the wine."

Miles and Bruce showed up at five thirty. True to his promise, Miles carried a nice bottle of white. Josie, who had pumped enough milk for the night, felt downright giddy at the sight of that wine.

"Open that," she commanded, slapping a corkscrew into the palm of his free hand. "Now. I can't even remember the last time I had a glass of wine."

It was so great to hang out with him, so easy and companionable. As good in its own way as having her sisters and beloved aunt around to share a hearty meal and a long talk.

Davy woke up as she set the food on the table. "Go back to sleep," she muttered under her breath. "Please…"

But he didn't. The fussy cries quickly turned to yowling.

"I'll get him." Miles headed for the front bedroom, returning with the wailing bundle that was her son. "This young man is starving."

"I'm on it." She filled a bowl half-full of water she'd kept warming on the stove. Miles walked the floor with Davy, patting his back, soothing him, as Josie took a bottle of her milk from the fridge and held it upright in the warmed water long enough to bring it to room temperature.

"Okay," she said as she switched the sealed cap for one with a nipple. "Pass him to me."

"I know how to feed this guy." Miles held out his big hand. She gave him the bottle and he took his seat at the table. With a final, furious yelp, Davy latched on to the offered nipple and got to work.

Josie sat down, too. "Silence," she murmured gratefully as she poured herself more wine.

Miles, his adoring gaze on Davy, nodded. "It almost makes the screaming worth it."

"No, it doesn't. Not even close." She sipped her wine slowly, savoring it. "This wine is so good. Thank you, Miles. Lately, I've been wondering if I would ever get a glass of wine again...and I don't mean just a taste. I mean a glass, maybe two. Enough for a buzz. Dear Lord, how I have missed the hazy joy of a wine buzz."

Miles whispered something to Davy.

Josie leaned back and spoke to the ceiling. "Here I'm hoping for a little adult conversation— scratch that. It doesn't even have to be 'adult.'" She air-quoted the word, then grabbed her glass again and raised it high. "Just another human being using actual words to communicate with me. That's all I need now. And the guy eating my chicken cacciatore would rather talk to my baby…"

Miles laughed again, the sound warm and wonderfully reluctant as ever. "Okay, okay. What did you want to talk about?" He balanced Davy and his bottle with one hand and used the other to grab his fork.

"Didn't I just say it doesn't matter what you talk about? Words, Miles. Words from the mouth of another human. That is what I crave."

Miles ate a big bite of chicken followed by a forkful of polenta and groaned. "Damn, woman. You really can cook. Marry me."

She snort-laughed. "And ruin a perfectly good friendship?"

"I might risk anything for food like this." He ate another bite.

"Yeah, well. Probably not that. Friendship is forever. Men and women and love and all that complicated stuff? Not necessarily."

He watched Davy, who was sucking at the bottle contentedly now. "I was surprised the night Davy arrived."

"To find me on your doorstep? I noticed."

"Yeah, that. But also when you said you chose a sperm bank to get pregnant."

"What?" She faked a scowl. "You don't approve?"

"It's not that. It's just, you've got it all, Josephine LeClaire. The looks and the big heart. You cook, you're a true farmer and you're also an excellent vet, the one to call when a fine mare suffers a prolapsed uterus after a difficult birth."

"Try not to use the word *uterus* at my dinner table."

He grinned. "You know what I mean. You're the whole package."

"Yes, I am," she agreed, seeing no need for false modesty on her second glass of wine. "Men, on the other hand…"

"Yeah?"

"Mostly, they're more trouble than they can possibly be worth—romantically speaking, I mean." She should probably leave it at that.

But that glass and a half of really nice white had loosened her tongue enough to make her likely to say things she might regret later. Also, Miles looked at her as though he really wanted her to go on, wanted to know how things had been for her, when it came to the male half of the species.

She started babbling, telling the poor man way more than he ever needed to know, talking about her first serious boyfriend, Justin Prebly. "You probably don't remember him. Justin moved here my junior year. By senior year, we became inseparable. I just knew it was forever with me and

Justin…" She explained how they'd planned to get married, her and Justin, right after graduation.

"And then I got pregnant," she confessed. "I couldn't make myself tell him. Finally, at a party on graduation night, I broke the big news. Justin held me and kissed me and told me it was all going to work out, that we would get married as planned, that he loved me more than life…"

"So you've been married, then?" Miles set Davy's empty bottle on the table.

"Hardly. The next day, Justin wouldn't take my calls. After a week of him blocking me, I went to his house. Nobody was there. I knocked and rang. I came back several times. And then one of my girlfriends said he and his family had moved away."

"Unbelievable," said Miles.

"I never saw him or any of the Preblys again."

"And the baby?" he asked solemnly, lifting Davy to his shoulder.

"I decided to keep it. Auntie M and my sisters completely supported me. But then, a few weeks later, I miscarried…"

"Josie." Miles held her gaze across the table. "I'm so sorry."

"Thanks. It was rough, but I got through it, undaunted love-wise, determined to try again, to finally find the man for me."

Davy started fussing. "Here," she said. "Finish your dinner. I'll change him."

"I don't mind." He started to rise.

"Sit down. Eat." She rose and took the baby from him. In the back bedroom, on the roomy new changing table with the beautiful shelves above it, she cleaned Davy up. He seemed drowsy, so she took him to her room and put him in the bassinet. He shut his eyes with a soft little sigh.

She washed her hands in the bathroom and then emerged into the main room again.

Miles asked, "No problems?"

"None. He went right down and straight to sleep." She took her seat across from him. They chatted about nothing in particular as Miles ate a second helping of chicken.

When he'd finished, he cleared off their empty plates. She served him apple pie with ice cream, and they split the last of the wine.

"So," said Miles, "after what happened with that jerk named Prebly, you tried again?"

"I did. Repeatedly." She regaled him with more stories of her various adventures in dating.

He said, "I could swear you went out with Taylor Brentwood for quite a while—that guy who used to own the bookstore on Central Street?"

"I did go out with Taylor, and as far as I know, he still owns Brentwood Books."

"So what happened there?"

By then, they'd finished their pie. She put the dishes in the dishwasher, and he took the dogs out for a few minutes while she brewed coffee.

When he came back in, they moved to the sofa.

"Come on now," he coaxed. "Tell me about Taylor Brentwood."

Josie kicked off the soft shoes she wore in the house, gathered her legs up to the side and leaned toward him. "Taylor and I dated exclusively for five years. Then he broke it off. He said we were in a rut. Three months later, he eloped with someone else."

Miles actually groaned. "What a jackass."

"My sentiments exactly." She offered the flat of her hand and they high-fived in agreement over the jackassery of Taylor. "That was two years ago, when Taylor and I broke up. After that, I just felt done, you know? Done with men and all their crap—present company excluded, of course."

"Good save." He had a sip of his coffee and set the mug on the sofa table. They grinned at each other. And then he prompted, "But you still wanted a family...?"

"I did. And that's why I decided on IUI." He looked kind of puzzled, so she clarified. "Intrauterine insemination—aka, the sperm bank."

"I see." He leaned toward her now, too. She realized she liked the way his thick, straight hair fell over his forehead, the way he wore it just a little too long so the ends of it caught on his collar. She liked his commanding nose—it was a lean nose, often called hawklike in novels she'd read. He smelled like plain soap and something else— cedar shavings, maybe. Or the deep woods, all cool and shady on a summer day? It was a scent both clean and manly.

And she felt so good in this moment, sharing this comfortable silence with him. "Miles?"

"Yeah?"

"Thank you."

"Anytime." The crease between his eyebrows told her he had no idea what she was thanking him for.

"You want to know why I'm thanking you?"

"Yeah. Yeah, I do."

"Well, let's start with the obvious. You saved the day when Davy was born. And then you came to my rescue again after Auntie M and my sisters returned to their lives. You made gorgeous shelves for Davy's room and then spent a whole day painting and putting that room together. And now, tonight, you brought the wine, fed my baby and listened to my long, sad story of disappointments in love."

"It wasn't that long of a story," he teased.

"Yeah, it was. But look at it this way, at least my story has a happy ending named David Miles."

"Yes, it does," he agreed.

She caught her lower lip between her teeth and worried it a bit before sharing more than she probably should have. "I think I just felt that I'd lost at love one too many times, you know? That I couldn't trust a man enough anymore to risk that kind of loss again."

He sat back away from her a fraction. His eyes seemed distant all of a sudden.

She reached out and brushed the sleeve of his soft wool shirt. "I'm sorry. I think I said way too much."

"No." His broad chest rose and fell with each slow, careful breath. "I just get it, what you said. I kind of feel the same way about loving someone, to be truthful."

Everything went quiet, like the world was holding its breath. She needed to keep her mouth shut. But she didn't. "Have you, um, dated, since Fiona died?"

His eyes still had that faraway look. But he answered frankly, "A few one-night stands, that's all."

"Ah," she said, because she had no idea what else to say. *Change the subject, fool*, she thought wildly.

But before she could come up with a suitably comfortable new topic, he went on. "I hated it, the whole app thing. Meeting some stranger at a bar for a night in a hotel room while my girls were with their grandmother." He laughed, a laugh that sounded more like a snort of self-derision. "I mean, I like sex as much as the next guy, but the whole thing just felt all wrong. I was never a one-night-stand kind of guy."

"So maybe you ought to try actual dating? Dinner and a show. Get to know the woman first."

"Josie. I'm not going to date. Not ever. It's what you said about yourself. I don't have it in me anymore to trust a woman, to risk the pain when it all goes to hell."

She had the powerful urge to tell him not to give up, that Fiona might have been his one and only, but he wasn't dead yet. It would in no way disrespect his wife's memory to learn to love again.

But really, what did she know? She'd yet to find true love in the first place.

"I can see how trying to get something going with someone new feels all wrong to you," she said. "I mean, you and Fiona always seemed so much in love. I can't imagine how horrible it must have been to lose her."

He laughed at that, an angry laugh. "Sorry, Josie. You've got it wrong."

She realized her mouth was hanging open and she snapped it shut. "I, uh, I do?"

He scoffed. "You do."

"How so?"

"You don't really want to know." His voice had icicles dripping from it.

Yes, she did want to know. She wanted to understand. "Try me."

Dead silence. And then his mouth curved in a cold, distant smile. "It's like this. Fiona was having an ongoing affair with another man the whole time we were married."

He could have hit her with a hammer, and she would not have been this stunned. "But...you *loved* her. Anyone could see it. You were happy with her right up to the end."

"Yes, I was. I was the dumbass husband who didn't have a clue what was going on."

Josie had no idea what to say, so she kept her mouth shut.

As for Miles, he planted his feet flat on the floor. Bracing his elbows on his spread knees, folding his hands between them, he stared off toward the fireplace on the opposite wall and continued, "I thought we were happy. I thought I had it all, the love of my life, two beautiful children..." He blinked and turned his head to look right at her. "You don't need to hear any of this."

She didn't?

Maybe not. At least part of her longed to unknow it, to hold on to the pretty fantasy that her neighbor and his wife had been happy together and deeply in love.

But already, in the short time since Davy's birth, she'd come to value this friendship that she and Miles were building. He'd been right there when she needed him, ready to do whatever she asked of him. Somebody needed to be there for him.

It just felt wrong for her to say anything, but… "Miles. Talk to me. Please. I'm listening."

He sent her a glance and then quickly looked away. "She'd been with that other guy since before she met me and I never had a clue until the day of her funeral, until after the interment, after everyone left."

"Oh, no…"

"Yeah. My mom took the girls home with her, so that I could have a few moments alone by her grave. I knelt there, by her headstone, whispering to her, telling her how much I loved her, how I would go on for our daughters' sake, but I would spend the rest of my life missing her, loving her, waiting for the day I could be with her again."

He shifted beside her and leaned back against the cushions. "In the middle of all that, while I was carrying on about how wonderful she was and how much I missed her, I heard a car door slam. I glanced up and saw a stranger in a designer suit and one of those fancy overcoats straight out of some arty Italian film. He was getting out of a limousine.

"That stranger came right to me. He stopped across her grave from me, tears running down his face. He said his name was Andrew Walker and he'd come to pay his respects. He said his heart was broken at the loss of *his* Fiona.

"*My* Fiona," Miles snarled. "That's what he called her. He babbled on, about how he'd been married to someone else, married before I even met the woman I thought was mine forever. He said he'd never been willing to divorce his wife, so Fiona married me. He said that, even though she'd stayed married to me for all those years and had my children, the love *he* had with Fiona had never died, that they'd been seeing each other in secret the whole time she was my wife."

Miles blinked and shook his head. "I didn't believe a word of it. I defended Fiona's memory by punching the crazy rich man in the face." With a hard huff of breath, he sat forward again and hung his head.

Josie almost put her arm around his wide shoulders.

But she stopped herself. She had a feeling he wouldn't welcome her touch—or anyone's right now, for that matter. "Oh, God, Miles. Could you just, maybe, tell me he was lying?"

He shot her a dark glance and then went back to staring at the fireplace. "Days passed. I couldn't stop thinking about what Andrew Walker had said. I thought about how Fiona had always traveled so much for work, how really, I had no idea what she actually did while she was gone. Finally, I started looking for clues…and I found them."

"You found proof that she was seeing him behind your back?"

He nodded. "There were letters. Letters from him. She'd saved them, squirreled them away in a locked drawer of her little desk in the great room. I found the key on the key ring in her purse. There were souvenirs, too, tickets and brochures from the places they went together. I burned that proof. All of it. Until it was nothing but ashes." He turned his head her way and met her eyes. "I'm nothing short of a refugee from *The Steve Wilkos Show.*"

"That's not true."

"Yeah, it is. And it gets worse, Josie. That bastard had said right to my face that Ash and Hazel were mine, that Fiona had had *my* children. Still, I doubted, you know?"

"Well, why wouldn't you doubt? There is no reason you should have believed anything he said."

"I did DNA on my own daughters, Josie. I pretended it was so they could learn more about their roots. But the truth was, I couldn't take it. I had to know for sure that the man my wife cheated on me with—the man she loved before me and kept on cheating with right up until her death—hadn't also fathered my daughters."

Josie had no idea what to say to him. She needed words that would comfort him, words to make him see that his reactions were exactly what anyone would feel in the position he'd found himself in.

He said, "The tests proved they're both mine. Too bad knowing that didn't make it all better for me. Instead, I despised myself."

"Miles, you did nothing wrong."

"Yes, I did. I just *had* to know, so I lied to them. I made it seem like some fun family project. I shouldn't have done that. I didn't even think it through. What if it had turned out I wasn't their biological father? What would I have done then? Broken their hearts all over again after they'd already lost their mother? Would I have had an obligation to find that cheating jackass, to introduce them to the man who'd provided half their DNA?"

"But none of that happened."

"Because I got lucky."

"God, Miles. Don't blame yourself for having to know. Anyone would want to know."

"I screwed up. And then I got lucky. The results came back the way I wanted them to. But that doesn't make me any less at fault. I could have hurt them so bad. And for what? Even if it had turned out they didn't share my DNA, Ash and Hazel are still mine and they always will be."

"Yes," Josie said, her voice steady and strong, though her vision had blurred with unshed tears. "Yes, of course, they are. And even if it had turned out that one or both of them wasn't biologically yours, you wouldn't have loved them any less. You would have worked through it with them. Miles, you are not the bad guy here. Stop torturing yourself. You did the best you could with a rotten situation."

He looked straight at her, into her eyes, seeking something—forgiveness, maybe. Peace. "I thought I had the great love, you know? She was anything but. She betrayed me, betrayed all we had together, from the first moment I met her until she kissed me goodbye that last time as she headed out the door for her morning run."

"Oh, Miles, I'm so, so sorry..."

"Don't be." His face went blank, his eyes ice-cold. "It's not like I deserve your pity."

"What? It's not pity. I care for you. You're a good man. You're the kind of friend I'm grateful to have in my corner."

He stared into the middle distance. "Two years ago, I threw out every single thing in our bedroom. I bought everything new—the bed, the lamps, the chairs, the curtains, the bedding. All of it. I wanted her gone. I didn't even want to sleep in the bed where she used to sleep."

"That's—" she sought the next word carefully "—understandable."

Miles didn't answer. He lowered his head and stared at the floor.

She spoke gently, soothingly. "Come on. Beating yourself up for finding a way to cope with a terrible betrayal isn't going to do anyone any good."

"Maybe not. But I'm not happy with myself, if you hear what I'm saying." He brought his hands up and wrapped them, fingers splayed, on either side of his skull, as though he feared his head might explode. In a hushed, broken voice, he said, "I can't believe I just told you all that."

"Miles, it's okay."

"No, it's not. I never told anyone any of that. Nobody ever needs to know that. I don't know what made me lay it all on you. I'm sorry."

"Don't be. *I'm* not sorry you talked to me. Miles, I really do feel that we've become friends. And sometimes it helps to talk to someone. I'm *glad* you told me. I think it's *good* that you told me. And I'll never say a word about it to anyone, I promise you that."

"You think it's good?" He made a rough, disbelieving sound low in his throat.

She felt his complete withdrawal acutely and

she couldn't stand it, couldn't stop herself from reaching out. She needed to make contact, to convince him that he could trust her, that it was all right to need comfort, that he could count on her to keep any secrets he shared with her.

He wasn't having it. Ducking away from her touch, he lurched to his feet. "It's getting late. I should go."

She jumped up, too. "Miles, please. Wait..."

But he was already striding around the coffee table, headed for the door. Pausing to click his tongue at his dog, he grabbed his coat off the peg and pulled the door wide. Bruce eased around him and went out first.

Miles turned back to her and pinned her with a look. "Forget what I said, okay?"

As if forgetting was actually an option. "Of course," she lied. "Whatever you need. And please stay. Sit down. We can talk a little bit more. We can—".

He cut her off. "I have to go."

But..." Before she could figure out what to say next, he went out. She was left staring at the door as he shut it behind him.

Chapter Five

Miles didn't come back.

He didn't call or send her a text to let her know he was okay. Not on Wednesday or Thursday or Friday, either.

Friday night, she couldn't take it anymore. She texted him.

Just checking in. I understand if you don't want to talk to me, but if you could just let me know that you're okay I would really appreciate it.

An hour later, he replied. I'm okay. Please don't worry about me.

She knew she needed to respect his wishes. All right, then. Thanks for getting back.

No problem. You take care, Josie.

You, too.

And that was that. She had to be content knowing that he loved his daughters and would take care of himself for their sake, at least.

The weekend crawled by. It snowed on and off. Twice, she took Davy outside with her—to gather eggs and to work in the greenhouse. Getting out, even just for a little while, helped a lot.

And despite her concern for Miles, she felt better about everything in her life—because of him, because of his kindness to her, because of the time they'd spent together. He'd understood her. She wished she could have made him feel that she understood him, too—too bad she'd failed to make him see that.

And now it looked like their new friendship was over when it had barely begun. That hurt, to know the beginning of something special and then to have it abruptly snatched away.

Still, she thought of him with fondness and gratitude. He'd been there at just the right moment in her life, when she needed a friend to remind her of all the basic truths. That life goes on, that things can work out.

He'd helped her feel strong and capable, helped her to remember what she already knew—that she and Davy would be just fine even without her aunt and younger sister living a short stroll from her front door.

Sunday morning, she got phone calls. From Auntie M, Alex and Payton. She spent over an hour on the phone with each of them, catching up, laughing over dumb stuff, feeling connected to the ones she loved.

Hazel came by her cottage that afternoon. She'd been at the rescue barn, taking care of the kittens. She held Davy and talked about school. She seemed fine, not the least apprehensive, just her usual cheery self. Josie felt reasonably certain the girl had no clue that anything had gone wrong between her dad and Josie.

After Hazel left, Josie took Davy out to the greenhouse again. As she dug in the dirt with her baby warm and safe against her heart, she told herself it was probably for the best, the way Miles was avoiding her.

That she missed him and thought of him constantly should be a red flag for her. She could way too easily get attached and the last thing she needed was to go pinning her hopes on some man again—even a really good man like Miles. She was a romantic disaster and he'd been played so hard he might never recover. It couldn't go anywhere between them, anyway...

Josie set down her narrow trowel and ripped off her gardening gloves.

Go anywhere? Her and Miles?

Please.

She liked him. She wanted to be his friend. That was all. End of story.

Tuesday, both Hazel and Ashley showed up in the late afternoon. They took turns holding Davy.

When Hazel went out to visit the kittens, Ashley complained about Miles. "He just doesn't get it. He wants me at home more. It's like, I could die of boredom, you know? I love it in town. I love being with my friends. Dad just doesn't understand that I want my own life and it's not going to be on a farm."

Josie hugged her. "I get it—or I'm trying to. But you know me. I'm a farmer through and through. Nothing thrills me like the smell of manure in the morning."

Ashley groaned. "You did not just say that."

"Hey. The last thing I would ever do is move to town."

Ashley pouted. "You're just like him."

Was she? And why did the thought that she might be like Miles please her so much? "Be patient with him, Ash. He loves you and he wants you to have the life *you* want. But it's his job to make sure you're safe and well and doing all the boring stuff—eating right, finishing your homework, getting enough sleep."

"Ugh." Ashley tipped her head down and looked up at Josie from under the thick veil of her dark eyelashes. "If you would maybe talk to him for me…?"

"Bad idea."

"Why?"

"I make it a rule not to stick my nose into other people's business."

Ashley pouted some more, but then Hazel came back in and rhapsodized over her favorite kitten, how big the kitten was getting and how she wished she could take her home now. "Come out and see her, Ash. She's so cute and very smart!"

And Ashley gave Josie a hug and whispered, "Thanks for listening."

"Always," Josie replied, and the sisters went out together to pet the kittens in the rescue barn.

The cottage seemed too quiet after they left. Not for long, though. Davy woke up wailing and Josie wished for all that quiet again.

Thursday, she and Davy went to her doctor, who gave her a prescription for birth control and cleared her to have sex—too bad she had no one to have sex with. Davy got his first shots. That night, he fussed a lot. She rocked him and sang to him.

And instead of wishing for Auntie M or Payton or Alex to miraculously drop by and lift her spirits a little, Josie wished for Miles.

She missed him, missed her friend.

Saturday, she made two mixed-berry pies using fruit she'd prepped and frozen last summer. One pie, she took out to Clark because he worked hard and deserved a delicious homemade pie.

The other pie, she tucked into an insulated pie carrier. It wasn't that cold out, in the low fifties. But she bundled Davy up nice and cozy, anyway, put him in his car seat in the back of her Jeep Renegade and off they went to Halstead Farm.

Five minutes later, she parked in front of the Halstead house. Carefully juggling Davy, the diaper bag and the pie carrier, she mounted the steps to Miles's front door.

Out of habit, Miles glanced out the beveled glass in the top of the door before pulling it open.

Josie.

Pink-cheeked, with all those corkscrew curls piled loosely on top of her head, she had Davy with her and what looked like baked goods in her right hand.

She saw him through the glass and her full lips curved into a grin.

Damn. He'd missed her. He'd been aching to go

to her, but he'd let all the stuff he shouldn't have told her hold him back.

He pulled the door wide.

They grinned at each other.

And then they were both talking at once, saying the same things at the same time. "It's so good to see you."

"How have you been?"

"Fine, yes."

"Doing okay…"

"Everything's good."

Finally, he stepped back. "Get in here. Come on."

She crossed the threshold and he shut the door. In silence, they regarded each other—until she held up the padded container in her right hand. "I figured if I brought pie, you would have to let me in."

"Good thinking." He tried to say it lightly. But then he moved a step closer and spoke more quietly. "I just, well, I laid all that ugliness on you, and I felt so bad for doing that. You didn't need to hear it, didn't need to know all that."

"That's not true. Yes, I did need to know it. And I'm guessing you needed to tell me. I think that's what a friend is—someone who can listen and care and not judge when you tell them the stuff that's hardest to talk about."

"Maybe."

She stuck out her chin at him. "Definitely."

"I still felt like a chump, a whiny fool who doesn't know when to shut up."

"No." Those big eyes stayed locked on him. "You were honest. You weren't a chump—no way."

"I was. And then the longer I stayed away, the harder it got to make a move."

"I get it. It's okay," she said in a tender little voice that told him she really did mean that. "I've just missed you, that's all."

He wanted to touch her, put his hand on her soft cheek, feel the reality of her, here, with him, after a week and half that had felt like forever. Instead, he said in a rough whisper, "And I missed you."

She gave him a look both steady and serious. "So then, Miles. Can we be over it, please?"

"Yeah. I want that. Let's be over it."

He took the pie and the diaper bag from her and set them on the table by the door. Next, she passed the baby to him so that she could get out of her coat.

Davy stared up at him in that dazed way of little babies. "You got bigger, didn't you, David Miles?" Davy scrunched up his button of a nose and burped.

"In eleven days?" Josie scooped up the pie again. "He gained maybe eight or nine ounces, max."

He led her into the kitchen area and stopped at the table. "Only eleven days? It felt a lot longer."

"Yeah," she said, gently now, as she set the pie on the counter, then turned to face him again. "It kind of did…" And she smiled. He really did like Josie's smile. It made the kitchen seem brighter. "You're going to want coffee to go with this pie. Mind if I…?"

"Go for it." He sat down with Davy as she loaded up the coffee maker.

As usual, Ashley was off with her friends, but Hazel wandered in as the coffee was brewing. Bruce trailed in behind her and flopped down under the table, ready to lick it right up if one of them dropped a dab of filling or a hunk of crust.

Before taking her first bite of pie, Hazel reluctantly showed Josie her new braces. Miles had driven her to the orthodontist to have them put in the day before. "I'll be wearing them for a couple years, probably," she said, looking glum but resigned. "And right now, they hurt."

Josie said, "The pain won't last but you will be gorgeous forever."

"That's what I keep telling myself," Hazel mumbled.

Josie suggested, "Maybe you'd rather have a smoothie than pie." She sent Miles a questioning glance. "I'm guessing your dad has a blender and fruit in the freezer?"

He forked up his first bite of the fine-looking pie. "Of course, I do."

Hazel grabbed hold of her plate with both hands. "Don't you dare take my pie."

Josie laughed. "I should've brought ice cream, at least…"

Miles got up. Shifting Davy to one arm, he opened the freezer. "How about vanilla?"

From behind him, Hazel and Josie sang out, "Yes!" in unison.

Holding Davy on one arm and a carton of Tillamook vanilla bean in his free hand, Miles turned.

And right then, like a puzzle, built piece by piece until suddenly the pieces seemed to find where they belonged by themselves, Miles saw what could be.

Him and Josie, together. Happy. A team.

After three years of merely going through the motions of his life, he wanted more. He wanted this, what was happening right now. Him and Josie, Hazel and Davy—and Ashley, if he could get her to stay home long enough—together. Laughing. Eating pie on a Saturday afternoon.

No, he didn't want to be somebody's fated love, her one-and-only. He no longer believed in any of that stuff.

But he did want a true companion. He wanted someone beside him, day to day and at night, too. Someone to hold. Someone who laid it all out there, about her life, about her past relationships, the way Josie had done—while giving birth to Davy and then eleven nights ago, too.

He wanted someone sweet, smart and honest. Someone easy to talk to. Someone generous and kind.

Josie paused with a bite of pie halfway to her mouth. "What?" He smiled and shook his head. She chuckled. "Shut the freezer door, Miles. Bring that ice cream over here."

During the week that followed, Miles made a point to spend time with Josie and Davy every day. He dropped by her cottage, or he invited her over in the evening. He found ways to help out at Wild Rose Farm, dropping in on Clark Stockwell, getting to know the man a little, pitching in with the animals and with the usual ongoing repairs around the place.

When Josie tried to tell him he was doing too much, he waved a hand and reminded her that they were friends and neighbors. "You help me," he said. "I do the same for you."

That Friday after they got home from school, the girls packed their overnight bags and went to stay at his mother's for the weekend. As soon as they drove away, Miles headed for Josie's. But her cottage was dark. He knocked, but no one answered.

At home, he almost texted her, but no. He put his phone away.

Maybe tomorrow...

He was about to heat up some leftovers, but that just seemed sad somehow, sitting home alone eating leftover chicken-fried steak. Instead, he called Rafe to see if he might want to head over to town, to Truitt's Taphouse, where they had burgers and nachos and local beer on tap, with three flat-screens playing football, basketball and hockey nonstop.

"Half an hour," said Rafe. "Meet you there."

Miles suggested, "I was thinking I'd ask Clark Stockwell and Kyle Huckston, too."

"Sounds good," Rafe replied in his easygoing way.

Both Kyle and Clark showed up.

They had a few beers and Clark opened up a little about his ill-fated move to Bend. He'd been hot and heavy with a winery owner and moved down there to be with her.

"I thought it was the real thing," he said. "My mistake. She and I didn't have whatever it takes to make it long-term."

Kyle was nodding. "Been there."

"But now there's Olga," said Rafe.

Kyle didn't even attempt to hide his pleasure at the mention of his fiancée. "Oh, yes, there is. And that woman is more than worth the wait."

Olga Balanchuk worked as a barista in the coffee place just up the street from Truitt's. "We've set the date," Kyle announced. "We're getting married in that great old barn at Wild Rose on the Sunday right after Thanksgiving. You're all three invited."

Clark offered a toast. "Here's to you and Olga. Some guys have all the luck."

Kyle tipped his beer at Miles. "Heard you were there last month when Josie needed you. She told me all about it. You're a hero, she said." Rafe and Clark exchanged one of those looks. Like they knew more than either was saying.

Miles grumbled, "Whatever that look was, you two need to knock it off."

Frowning, Kyle glanced from Rafe to Clark and back to Rafe again. "Okay. There's a vibe. What's going on?"

Rafe set down his beer and put up both hands as if he was a robbery victim. "Don't fire me, boss. I didn't say a word…"

Clark grunted. "Come on, Miles. Josie LeClaire is terrific. And we all know the two of you have been spending a lot of time together."

"I didn't know." Kyle looked hurt. "How come nobody told me?"

"We're telling you now," said Clark and turned to Miles again. "Nobody will be the least surprised if you two end up together."

Now, all three of them were looking at him.

And Miles just went ahead and said what he was thinking. "Josie's special. It's a lucky man who gets a chance with her."

Kyle blinked like someone had flashed a bright light in his eyes. "Whoa, Miles. You and Josie..." He frowned. And then he shrugged. "I had no idea, but you know, it kind of makes sense..."

Rafe poked Miles with an elbow. "You should go for it, man. Just step right up. Stop messing around and make your move."

Late Saturday afternoon, Miles dropped by Josie's again.

She answered the door with Tink at her heels and a squalling Davy in her arms. "Miles! Come on in."

He reached for Davy, and she handed him over.

Ten minutes later, the baby had fallen asleep on his shoulder and Josie asked if he wanted to stay for dinner. "Call the girls," she suggested. "There's plenty."

"I would, but they're at my mom's for the weekend."

"Ah," she said with a tiny smile. "So it'll be just you and me, then?"

He held her gaze. "Yeah." On his shoulder, Davy made a soft huffing sound.

Josie said, "He's out. Put him to bed? I moved his bassinet into his beautiful new room..."

* * *

Feeling oddly giddy to have Miles all to herself for the evening, Josie was dishing up pork chops when he rejoined her in the kitchen. She pointed at a bottle of pinot noir that was waiting on the counter. "Open that. Corkscrew in the…"

He pulled the corkscrew out of the drawer before she could show him where to look.

She laughed. "It's official. You know what's in my drawers."

He frowned. "Why did that sound dirty?"

She stifled a silly giggle and sent him a sideways glance. "Just pour the wine."

He uncorked the bottle. "I came by yesterday afternoon but missed you."

"Yeah, I went to the feed store to pick up a few things. Took forever. Shopping can get really complicated when there's a baby involved."

He poured them each a glass and handed one to her. "Here's to you, Josie."

"And to you, Miles." She tapped her glass to his.

A few minutes later, they sat down to eat. The conversation flowed easily and she thought how grateful she was for his friendship.

They'd been spending a lot of time together in the last week and she'd enjoyed every minute of it. It was such a relief that they'd gotten past that rough patch after he told her the truth about Fiona. Now she felt closer than ever to him.

He did way too much for her, yes. But he really did seem to want to help her out. And she tried her best to repay his constant kindness, mostly with hot meals and baked goods.

As they were clearing the table, he said, "A toy cabinet would be a nice addition to Davy's room."

She rinsed a plate and put it in the open dishwasher. "Eventually, yeah. But he doesn't need one anytime soon."

"It's nice, though, to plan ahead, to have things ready." His voice was low and the way he looked at her...

It seemed intimate. Like maybe he was thinking of her as more than a friend.

Warmth bloomed low in her belly and a sweet shiver raced over her skin. He really was so attractive, so capable and serious, protective and helpful. And big and strong and...

What were they talking about?

She remembered—the toy cabinet. "Um. Yeah. Planning ahead never hurts." She grabbed the hand towel.

"I'm thinking it would look good against the wall across from the changing table. I could put one together so easily. It would take no time at all. Something simple, a box with shelves and cabinet doors—got a pencil and a scrap of paper?"

She stared at him, overly aware of the breadth of his shoulders, the fine, big shape of his hands, the intelligence in his blue eyes, the sexy curve of his mouth.

Snap out of it, Josephine.

Focus. She drew a slow, careful breath and hung the towel back on its hook. "Paper and pencil, you said?"

"Yeah." Really, the way he looked at her—like he knew something she didn't. Something good. Something special.

They went back to the table, where he sketched out the cabinet for her, marking the dimensions, showing how it would fit on the inside wall. "I wouldn't make it too deep, so you wouldn't lose much space in the room. I could do cubbies, with tubs or baskets if you'd rather."

"That might be better, with cubbies. Easier to just toss things in an open container of some sort. And I can get those bright-colored square bins…" She found herself leaning closer

He looked up.

And it just happened, like it was the most natural thing in the world. They leaned in as one, as though magnetized to each other.

"Miles?"

"Josie."

Their lips met. It felt so good, so absolutely

right, his mouth hot and soft against hers. She opened for him with a happy sigh.

Vaguely, she heard the scrape of his chair. He started to rise. She did the same.

His arms went around her. She melted against him.

Could this be happening?

Could it please never stop?

He lifted away…but only to come right back to her, settling that wonderful mouth on hers again. His body, hot and broad and hard against her, felt so right. Like something she'd been missing all her life.

His hands strayed upward. He cradled her face. "Josie…"

Her eyes had drifted shut. They felt heavy as she opened them and found him staring down at her, looking a little flushed, his lips deliciously swollen—from kissing her, of all things.

His palms felt wonderfully warm against her cheeks. A little rough from hard work, they skimmed down the side of her neck and outward. He clasped her shoulders.

For a moment, it all seemed unreal—the kiss that had thrilled her, the soft look in his eyes. Any second now, that soft look would vanish. He would turn and run. She would be staring at the back of him again as he walked out her door.

But then he leaned down enough to press his

forehead to hers. "Despite all that stuff I probably shouldn't have told you, there are things I really miss about being married."

"Yes, you *should* have told me," she chided in a voice so husky and low it hardly sounded like her own. "That's what friends are for."

"To dump all your emotional garbage on?"

"It was not garbage. And sometimes you just need to be able to talk about the painful things with someone who won't judge. Someone who won't betray your confidence. Someone who's just going to listen and not tell you what to do or how you should feel."

He touched her cheek again, the barest breath of a touch this time. The slight contact sent a ripple of sensation all through her body. "I'm glad you're my friend, Josie."

"Me, too. Now, what do you miss about marriage?"

His gaze never strayed from hers. "I miss the feeling of partnership, the belief that I can count on the other person. I miss having someone to talk to—or I did miss those things. Until lately. With you."

"Miles..." It seemed the only word she knew right at that moment.

He said, "I miss sex with someone I care about."

Really, he did smell wonderful. She leaned

in close again and nuzzled her nose against his shirt—laundry soap and man. A heady combination. "Well, Miles. I've never been married. The times I've been in love, it didn't end well. I have to admit, I don't trust the romantic kind of love. I don't want it. I really don't. Romantic love has always disappointed me. I don't trust the big, overblown emotions."

"I feel the same." He licked his lower lip and arched one eyebrow.

Her belly felt all warm and heavy. She confided, "As for sex with someone I care about, yeah. I miss that, too. And you know..." She hesitated, not sure if she should say the rest.

"Tell me," he commanded, but his voice was gentle and low.

"We would make a great couple if only we didn't have to fall in love."

He laughed at that, and she laughed with him. Tenderly, he combed her hair with his fingers. Her curls resisted him. He ended up guiding a thick swatch of spiraling coils behind her ear. "I want you to think about it."

"About...?"

"You. Me. How we might be, together."

With her midsection melting and her skin dying for his touch, thinking didn't come easy. "How is this happening? I mean, I had no idea that kissing you would be so..."

"So…?"

She laughed at the sheer absurdity of life, of right now, of kissing Miles and discovering she couldn't wait to kiss him again. "We're friends, Miles. That matters to me. I don't want to mess with that."

"Neither do I." He stepped back. She had to resist the need to grab him and yank him in close again. "Think about it." He took her left hand and gently stroked her ring finger, circling it with the fingers of his right hand.

Her breath tangled in her throat at the odd, sweet caress. "I will. Yes…"

"All right then." He picked up the drawing he'd made of the toy cabinet and stuck it in his pocket.

She watched him cross the room and put on his coat.

Then he turned to her. "Tomorrow night? Have dinner with me at Barone's." Barone's was a Heartwood landmark. They served really good Italian food in a quiet, cozy setting.

Dinner out. With Miles. She hadn't been out to dinner with a man in forever, not since long before she got pregnant with Davy. "I would love to, but what about Davy?"

"Would you trust Hazel to babysit him?"

"Of course. She was always amazing with Payton's boys. But it would be the first time he's been away from me. We couldn't be gone for too long."

"We can always bring the food home if he doesn't do well—or if you find you're not ready to be away from him."

Was she ready? Her baby *was* seven weeks old. "What about Hazel? You said she's in town with her grandmother."

"She and Ash will be home tomorrow afternoon. I'll check with her in the morning and let you know."

First thing the next morning, Miles called Hazel.

She had her own phone now, one he'd bought her for her thirteenth birthday, and she answered on the second ring. "Hey, Dad."

"Hey, Haze." He got right to the point. "Feel like babysitting tonight? I asked Josie to have dinner at Barone's with me."

"Whoa, Dad. You're going out with Josie?" She actually giggled.

And he felt instantly uncomfortable. "Is that somehow funny?"

"No, I just… Well, Dad. I think that's cool. It's only that you never date."

He almost started arguing with her about the word *date*. Was it a date? He supposed that it was. After Fiona's treachery, he'd never planned to date anyone again. But then, he'd never planned to get married again, either.

His friendship with Josie had changed everything. "The question is, would you be willing to watch Davy tonight?"

"Daddy…" Hazel spoke gently, though a hint of humor still lingered in her voice. "I would love to watch Davy tonight."

Why did he suddenly feel younger than the thirteen-year-old on the other end of this call? "Ahem. Good, then. I'll let Josie know."

"Dad?"

"Hmm?"

"I really love that you're going out with Josie. I think Josie's amazing. And I've been waiting for her to ask me to babysit Davy."

He mumbled something awkward and halting and resisted the temptation to warn her not to say anything to her grandmother—after all, if tonight went as he hoped, his mother would find out about him and Josie very soon, anyway. "Thanks, sweetheart. See you at two."

He called Josie next. "Good morning."

"Hi." Did she sound kind of breathless?

Grinning for no reason at all, he stared out the front window over the kitchen sink. "We're on for tonight. Hazel will watch Davy. Be ready at six?"

"I will. See you then."

Five minutes after he hung up, his mother's name flashed on the screen. Resigned, he took the call. "Hi, Mom."

Donna Halstead wasted no time getting straight to the point. "It's about time you asked a nice woman out, a nice girl, someone we all know and like. You and Josie have so much in common. Both farmers, both single parents. And Josie is really quite impressive, now, isn't she? I mean, she runs that farm herself, takes care of her new baby—and she's a veterinarian, too. She has a lot on her shoulders. Sometimes I wonder how she does it all."

"She's taken a break from the animal clinic, just for a few months, I think, until Davy's a little older."

"Well, I'm glad to hear it. Even someone like Josie can only do so much—and I'll say it again. As for your going out with Josie, I do believe that I approve."

"I'm so glad to hear that, Mom." And he *was* glad. His life was always easier when his mother approved.

"And the girls tell me that the baby is adorable."

"Yes, he is."

"And Josie even gave him your name for his middle name. Clearly, you bonded, the two of you, when that baby was born."

"Uh, we did. Yes."

"That she went to a sperm bank is a little…different. But not in a bad way. I mean, it's great that the father won't be an issue."

"Who told you that Josie went to a sperm bank?"

"Hazel, of course."

So Hazel did know about the sperm bank. Josie *had* told her. Did Ashley know, too? Was he the most clueless dad on the planet? Possibly. He should have checked with Josie on the subject long before now.

Donna instructed, "When the time is right, you should consider adopting little David."

He fully intended to do more than *consider* it—not that his mother had any say in the matter. "Mom. I love you. Back off."

"Take Josie somewhere nice."

"I will, Mom."

"And have a wonderful time."

He promised he would and then she let him off the phone without once complaining about Ashley. Miles decided to call that a win. He glanced at his phone again, checking the time. It was pretty early. He could muck out a few stalls in the horse barn before cleaning up and heading for Portland, where more than one jewelry store opened at eleven, Tiffany's included.

Miles had never been to Tiffany & Co. in his life. But even if this wasn't about hearts and flowers and love ever after, it mattered. Josie needed to know how highly he valued her. That he didn't view her lightly. He respected her. He'd chosen her, even though, after Fiona, he'd been certain he would never choose anyone again. And in choosing her, he truly hoped she would choose him back.

What he wanted—what he had planned if things worked out for the two of them—was about real life, and trust, about building a future with someone he could believe in, someone who valued the kind of life that he valued.

A ring might be just a symbol. But he wanted her to love the ring he selected for her. He wanted her to have the best.

Chapter Six

"Dinner out," Josie said dreamily after they'd been seated in a cozy booth at Barone's and the waitress had left to bring them wine and appetizers. "I can't believe this is happening." She beamed across the table at Miles. "If this is a dream, please don't wake me up."

Miles really did like looking at her, at those big, trusting eyes, those cute freckles and that soft mouth he wanted to kiss again. "It's real, Josie. I promise you." *And about to get more real.*

But he needed to lead up to that properly, to choose the perfect moment. It would be a practical arrangement, but he wanted to make it crystal clear how much he liked her. He wanted to be sure she understood that she really did matter to him.

And in the meantime, he might as well have the sperm-bank conversation. "I keep wanting to ask you..."

Right then, the waitress returned with wine and bread. She opened the bottle. He tasted it and nodded his approval.

When she left again, Josie dipped a hunk of bread in olive oil and balsamic vinegar. "Ask me what?"

"Well, it's like this. When I called Hazel this morning to ask if she would watch Davy, my mother did what she always does and listened in...and then she called me back. She instructed me to take you somewhere nice. She also brought up that you used a sperm donor. She said Hazel had told her so."

Josie chuckled. "Let me guess. Your mom's matchmaking us?"

"She likes you. She's glad I'm hanging around with a 'local girl everybody likes'—her words."

"I like your mom." She slanted him a look from under her lashes. "But I have noticed that Donna has a definite opinion on every little thing."

"There's no denying that. But I did want to check with you—and you're good, then, with my just telling people that you used a donor?"

"Well, yeah. It's what I did."

"I'm with you. But I didn't know if maybe it was something you would rather tell people yourself."

She set down the bit of bread she'd been nibbling on. "You're a thoughtful guy, Miles."

"Thoughtful." He turned the word over in his mind, checking it for flaws. "That's good, right?"

She grinned. "Yes, it is. Very good."

"Well, thank you. When it comes to my girls, I'm mostly stumbling around in the dark, missing all the cues, trying to catch up with whatever's going on with them."

She reached across the table and took his hand. Hers felt cool and soft and small in his big paw. "You're a great dad, Miles. The best." Warmth spread through him at her words. He wanted to kiss her, to pop the question right then and there.

But before he could get started telling her how highly he regarded her and what a great team they would make, she went on, "Anyone who asks, just tell them the truth. I wanted a baby and I decided to have one all on my own. That's what I told Ashley when she asked me. Hazel, too. They were sweet, both of them. Concerned for me. Wondering if I'd been dumped by some coldhearted douchebag. I explained that I hadn't." She leaned in and lowered her voice to a more intimate level, just between the two of them. "Not this time, not with Davy, anyway…"

He remembered her story about that guy back in high school, about the baby she'd lost after that creep ran out on her. Thinking about that heartless jerk made him want to get up and slide over to her side of the booth, to wrap his arm around her and tell her how terrific she was.

He would have done it, too. But right then, the waitress showed up with their appetizers. Josie eased her hand from his grip and exclaimed over how delicious it all looked.

They ate. They talked about feed prices. She said her sister Payton would come down from Seattle next week with the twins. Payton still pitched in with farm business remotely. She managed the farm's website and helped manage special events. Next weekend, Payton had meetings with two June brides who would be getting married at Wild Rose in the barn the sisters had fixed up for weddings, parties and farm-to-table dinners, the barn where Kyle Huckston would marry Olga Balanchuk the Sunday after Thanksgiving.

The main course arrived. The conversation flowed, easy and natural, between them. Inside, though, he was a ball of nerves.

How to ask. *When* to ask...

He should have thought this through better. He didn't really even know how to start with this.

It had all been so different with Fiona. Looking back, he realized now that Fiona had run that show, from start to finish. She'd chosen him to make a life with because Andrew Walker refused to divorce his wife. They'd met in the bookstore when he was at Portland State. She'd asked him out, treated him like a king, told him she loved him madly and always would. He'd believed he was the luckiest man in the world. Suddenly, without his even having to think about it, he and Fiona had decided to get married. At the time, it had seemed so natural, so right, like it was all his idea...

The waitress cleared off their plates. "How about some dessert?"

Five minutes later, they were eating Barone's famous ricotta-and-cinnamon trifle with salted amaretto and finishing the last of the wine.

"It was so good, Miles," Josie said as they crossed the parking lot to his crew cab. "I think that trifle changed my life..." They reached the passenger door and he pulled it open for her. She cast a glance at the sky. "It's a beautiful night." And it was, clear and cold, with the stars looking close enough to reach up and touch.

It was also damn near over and he hadn't said a word about the two of them and the future and what he hoped they could have together.

He caught her arm as she started to climb in. "Wait..."

"Hmm?" She turned those big eyes up to him.

And that did it. "Josie..." He kissed her.

She tasted like their fancy dessert, and she felt just right, her round breasts pressing into his chest, her arms twining eagerly around his neck. He could hold her forever and never let go. He loved that he ached for her at the same time as he knew he could trust her.

Never had he expected to let himself trust a woman again.

But Josie was different. She told the truth and she said what she actually thought. There was no pretense in her. No hidden agenda. If she would have him, they could be friends and lovers and partners in running their two farms. They would work side by side to make a better life for each other and their children.

"I've been wanting to kiss you all night," he whispered as he lifted his mouth from hers.

"Oh, Miles. Me, too," she replied as he slanted his lips the other way and kissed her again.

It was perfect, him and Josie, standing in Barone's parking lot next to his truck under a blanket of stars, kissing like a couple of crazy kids who couldn't get enough of each other. He slipped his hand inside her coat. She moaned when he brushed his palm against the soft outward curve of her breast.

"Josie..."

"Miles..." She tipped her head to the side, inviting him. He kissed his way down the long, silky column of her throat and back up again, breathing in the scent of her, sweet as a basket of flowers, wanting to stand here beside his truck forever, just holding her.

Kissing her.

He took her face between his hands.

Her eyes met his. "I really like kissing you," she whispered. "I like it so much…"

He kissed her one more time, hard and fast. "Better get in the truck." She jumped up to the seat. He shut the door, went around to the driver's side and got in behind the wheel. "I suppose you need to get home…"

She nodded. "I should, yeah. It's his first time with a sitter…and mine, too."

"All right, then." He turned on the engine.

But before he could shift into gear, she put her hand on his arm. "You'll have to take Hazel home…"

"Right."

"It's awkward, huh? For me to ask you to sneak out of your own house tonight?"

"You have no idea how much I want to do just that. It's not as though the girls aren't old enough to be alone for a few hours. And they know I took you to dinner…"

"But if you left, you would feel you should tell them where you're going."

"Yeah."

She gave him a slow smile. "You don't want to explain to Hazel and Ashley that you need to run over to Wild Rose Farm and kiss me some more."

He laughed. "You're right. I'm a coward—with the girls, with my mother."

She leaned in. So did he. They shared another slow, sweet kiss. He was having such a great time. He didn't even care that he hadn't found the moment to pop the big question, that he'd yet to bring out the little velvet box waiting in his coat pocket. He had a goal, a reasonable, workable plan for the two of them, and he really wanted to get going on that, on the rest of their lives.

But just being with Josie was turning out to be so much fun.

Fun. How long had it been since he'd simply had fun? Sometimes, looking back, it seemed to him he'd had no fun at all with Fiona. He'd felt passionate and deeply in love with her, like he'd snared a rare prize in getting her for his wife. But they hadn't laughed together much, really.

She had her work traveling around northern Oregon and southern Washington as a pharmaceuticals rep. He'd had the farm. He'd told himself he had it all.

Looking back, though, he should have seen the cracks in the marriage he'd once considered perfect. It should have been obvious early on...at least by the time the girls came along. Fiona didn't like having to be home so much.

He'd wanted only to please her, so he'd talked to his mom. Donna would drive in from town every day to watch Ash and Hazel so that Fiona could get back to work. It had never occurred to him that his wife, the woman he considered the love of his life, might be busy with more than selling medicine to doctors and pharmacies.

"How about this," Josie said. "Come over tomorrow while the girls are in school, say around noon. I'll make us some lunch and we can have a little time together. If we happen to share a few kisses, it can be just between us. You don't have to explain yourself to your daughters."

He put his finger under her chin and lightly rubbed at her soft lower lip with his thumb. His life had felt so gray for so long. But then Josie had pounded on his door at three in the morning. When he'd found her crouched on his doorstep about to have Davy, he'd had no idea that the gray fog was already lifting, fading away.

"What?" she asked.

He kissed the end of her nose. "I do like the way your mind works."

"So, then. Tomorrow?"

"Tomorrow," he agreed and started up the truck.

* * *

Josie had plans for her afternoon with Miles. She would make him an offer and she fervently hoped it would be one he wouldn't refuse.

She spent extra time getting ready, choosing a silky top and her best jeans, the snug ones she'd finally managed to zip up a few days ago. She wore actual makeup—not a lot, but some blusher and mascara and lip color that made her mouth look even fuller than it was.

He showed up right at noon. She had the food waiting on the table, because she wanted to get lunch out of the way and move on to the good stuff. Miles took Davy and they sat down to pot roast with carrots and potatoes and warm bread.

She'd pumped right before he arrived. That way, he could give Davy a bottle, which he seemed to like doing, and she would have less chance of leakage should the afternoon unfold as she hoped it might.

He seemed quiet and she felt way too nervous. But he kept sending her intimate glances and warm smiles, so she didn't lose confidence in her plan.

When the meal was over, Miles took Davy into the back bedroom to change him. Tink trailed along after them. Lately, Tink had taken to snoozing in Davy's room whenever the baby slept.

Twenty minutes later, Miles came back out

alone. "I rocked him for a little. He went out like a light, and when I put him in the bassinet, he just settled right in, never opening his eyes."

She held out her hand to him. He took it and it felt right, his long fingers warm and solid, weaving between hers. "Let's sit down."

He followed her to the sofa, and they sat side by side.

"I've been thinking," she said, turning into him.

"Me, too." He leaned toward her.

"You first?" she offered.

He brought her hand to his mouth and brushed his soft lips across the back of it, causing all her nerve endings to quiver and burn. He'd shaved and his hair was slicked back, like he'd showered before he came over.

Was this really happening? It did seem that they might be on the same page here.

"No," he said, his voice kind of rough, all sexy and low. "You go ahead."

"Well, you might have noticed that I really like kissing you."

"I did notice." He eased an arm around her. She curled up nice and close to him with a happy sigh.

When his mouth met hers, she opened to him. That kiss went on for quite a while. When he lifted away a little, she went for it.

"So, Miles, we talked about how neither of

us is up for some big romance." She touched his cheek—so smooth now because he'd shaved just for her. "But with you, I feel good, you know? I feel that we get each other, that we're friends."

"*Good* friends," he added, and nuzzled her hair. "And I do want you, Josie."

Her breath felt all tangled up in her chest. "It means a lot. To hear you say that. I want you, too. And that's why I was thinking, we could maybe take a chance..."

He chuckled. The sound seemed to promise all manner of sexual pleasures. "Take a chance on...?"

She felt ridiculously young all of a sudden, full of bright hopes and new dreams and the magic of longing for a certain someone, the sheer, perfect agony of burning up with desire. "I don't know what to call it. Benefits? A secret affair...?"

He stroked a hand down the coils of her hair, smoothing it, though there really was no way to smooth hair like hers. His voice low and gravelly, he said, "I want benefits, with you."

Her heart seemed to grow larger inside her chest. "Yeah?"

"Oh, yeah." He caught her chin, tipped it up and covered her mouth with his own.

That kiss was endless. She drowned in the sweet, hot pleasure of it.

But then he pulled back—just enough to cradle

her face between his big hands as he asked, "But why not go for more?"

She blinked up at him, dazed with desire, wondering at his question. "More?"

He took her by the shoulders and held her away. "Stay right here."

"What? Wait, I…" She grabbed for him.

But he was already up and striding to the door. Lifting his jacket off the coatrack, he took something from the pocket and then returned to her.

She put her hand over her racing heart. "I thought you were leaving."

"No way." And then he pushed the coffee table back from the sofa and dropped to one knee in front of her.

"Miles?" she asked, her voice rising sharply. "What's going on?"

He held up a small velvet box and opened the lid. She gasped at the sight of a platinum ring set with diamonds all the way around the band—exactly the ring she would have chosen for herself, the kind a woman who worked with her hands could wear most of the time and not worry about snagging it on something.

"Josie LeClaire. I'm not a man to go for a secret fling. I want more."

A silly little squeak escaped her, and she asked again, "More?"

He gazed into her eyes, his focus unwavering.

"I trust you, Josie. I like you so much. And I can't stop wanting you all the time. No, I can't offer you love, whatever that really is, but you said you didn't want it. And I swear to you that I will give you everything else—everything. And in return, I would want the same from you. Your loyalty, your trust, your hand in mine for as long as we're both breathing. A good life, the kind of life we both want. A partnership of equals, you and me."

"You're asking me to...?"

"Marry me, Josie. Please make me happier than I ever thought I could be again. Say you'll be my wife."

Oh, sweet Lord.

It all sounded so good, Miles kneeling in front of her, holding up the perfect ring, offering all the things she'd stopped hoping for—a fine life with the right man. She could have all that with him.

Everything but...

Love.

The big word. The word that had always meant disappointment for her. She did not trust that word, not in the context of what went on between men and women.

Still, it felt just a little bit wrong, to marry someone without love, didn't it?

Really, wasn't marriage *about* love?

"Say yes," he commanded, his voice so calm, so sure. All man. And such a good man.

Why was she hesitating?

She knew she could trust him. They wanted the same things from life. Everything would be better, easier, richer, sweeter if the two of them became partners, a team—Miles and Josie together, taking on the world.

She loved his daughters, and he loved Davy. They would build a strong, loving family together. They would have each other, hold each other, take care of each other in all the ways that mattered most. She should jump at his offer.

And she probably would.

In a minute.

A little pondering wouldn't hurt, though. A decision like this was huge. If she wanted to take all the time in the world, well, she would.

She put up her index finger. "A minute…"

He understood. "You're right," he said quietly. "Think it over. Do you want me to go?"

"Don't you dare. Stay right here."

A smile tugged at the corners of his mouth. "All right then. Take as long as you need." His eyes never wavered. He waited for her answer, so steady, so certain and calm.

She could just see them, working together through the years. That he owned the farm next door to Wild Rose could not have been more perfect. They could count on each other from planting through harvest time and on into the winter, maybe talk about trying to get adjoining booths during Saturday market months. They might set up one big, joint farm stand out on the main road.

They would raise Davy together, and she would be there for the girls as they grew into the fine women they already promised to be. She and Miles might even think about having one more baby...

It would be the kind of life she'd given up dreaming about...until right now, after lunch on a sunny Monday afternoon, when she'd intended only to seduce him while Davy slept, and instead found him kneeling before her, asking her to be his wife.

No man had ever knelt for her...until this man. Until Miles.

The words rose in her throat, demanding to be said.

Josie let them free. "I care for you, Miles Halstead. I like you and I trust you and I want to be with you. So, yes. Please. Let's get married. Let's spend our lives together, you and me."

Chapter Seven

Yes! She'd said yes!

A bolt of triumph, hot and razor-sharp, shot through Miles. He wanted to jump up, grab her close and claim that soft, perfect mouth of hers, to sweep her up in his arms and carry her straight to bed.

But the moment deserved a little damn reverence.

He took the ring from the box and set the box on the coffee table. "Give me your hand."

"Yikes!" With a happy little giggle, she did as he asked.

He slipped the glittery band of diamonds onto her ring finger.

"Oh, Miles." Turning her hand this way and that, she admired the sparkle. "It's so beautiful. And a perfect fit..." She met his eyes again and her lips curved in a knowing smile. "Saturday night, just before you left, when you told me to think about how it might be, you and me..."

"What about it?"

"You made a circle of your fingertips on my ring finger. You were measuring for a ring, weren't you?"

"I've got a pretty good eye, but I wasn't sure until now that I'd gotten it right..."

"It's a perfect fit and I love it."

"Josie." He pulled her up with him as he rose. "Come here."

And then he had her in his arms, warm and soft and *his*. The feel of her was all he'd believed he would never have again.

It was everything he'd given up on—and also, so much more. Because he knew her. *Really* knew her. Knew her history and her family. She wasn't some stranger he'd met in the bookstore at Portland State. She'd grown up next door to him. He'd known her all her life.

"Josie..."

"Yes, Miles. Absolutely. Yes."

He took her mouth, kissed her deep and slow and thoroughly, feeling the soft length of her all along the front of him, aching to have her, not wanting to wait. She offered herself so freely. He wanted her naked, wanted to scoop her right up and carry her to her bedroom, to kiss every inch of her, to be inside her, the two of them moving together on the sheets of her bed.

Instead, he took her by the shoulders.

She made a desperate, hungry sound. "Don't pull away," she whispered, her beautiful mouth tipped up like an offering.

He kissed her again, instantly getting lost in the feel and the scent of her. The last thing he wanted to do was stop.

But he made himself pull back. He took a thick bunch of that untamed hair and wrapped it nice and snug around his fist. "I want you so bad…"

She groaned. "And that's good, Miles. That's very good…" Her clever fingers danced downward between their bodies. "I want you, too." She rubbed her palm against him. It felt so right. He ached to have her.

Now he was the one who couldn't hold in a gruff, needy sound. His body burned and his head spun. "But listen…"

"Hmm?"

"Josie, I want to get married soon."

"Soon is good," she said in a breathless little whisper. "Soon is perfect. I don't want a big wedding. Just us. The families. Short and sweet. It's the life we'll have that I want—a life together."

How did she do that? How did she so exactly understand him? How did they both want this to go the same way? He unwound her hair from around his fist and smoothed it gently. "I agree. I want to get started on our lives together."

"All right, then."

"And I want to wait to have sex with you until we're married."

Her eyes widened. "What? *Wait?*"

With a chuckle, he bent close again and nuzzled her cheek. Breathing her in, he rubbed his nose along hers. "God. You smell so good…"

"But you said you want to wait?" She sounded bewildered. Her breath came in eager bursts.

He nipped at her strong chin. "Yeah. I want to wait for our wedding night."

"Miles." She stopped driving him wild with that stroking palm of hers and slid her hand back up between them to cradle the side of his face. "That's totally unnecessary. Nobody waits for the wedding anymore."

"Some people do." He kind of growled the words. "What can I say? I'm an old-fashioned guy—and okay, I remember what I told you. We both know that since Fiona's death, I haven't always been celibate. But I never felt right about it. That's not who I want to be. I want you for my wife and I want to wait…just, you know, not too long."

She hummed low in her throat, a sound both sweet and sexy, a sound that sent a fresh bolt of desire searing through him. "All right. I could get behind that…"

He still burned to bury himself inside her, but he felt glad, too. That she really did seem willing to go along with him on this. "You sure?"

"Yes, I am. I'm sure." She stroked her palm around the back of his neck and eased her fingers up into his hair. "But there should be lots of kissing in the meantime."

"I'm all for kissing, anytime. All the time." He swooped down and took her mouth. The heat between them bloomed hotter than ever.

And when he lifted his head, she repeated, "Lots of kissing. And our wedding had better be soon."

That night after dinner, while Davy was napping, Josie called her aunt first and shared the big news.

Auntie M said, "You fell in love with Miles Halstead. Wonderful. I like him so much, always have. I know that you two will be so happy together."

A twinge of unease tightened the muscles between Josie's shoulder blades as her mind leaped to all the reasons it was okay that she and Miles weren't going to the love place. They had mutual respect and the same goals in life. They truly, deeply *liked* each other. And the chemistry between them was off the charts. "I can't wait to marry him. And guess what? We're not going to wait. Miles and I both want our wedding to be simple and soon."

Auntie M said, "I'm so happy for you, sweetheart. I'll be there within the next few days to help you put it all together..."

They talked for a while, sharing ideas for the wedding and also catching up on farm business. Auntie M wanted to know how it was going, how Josie was handling things now she had Davy to think about, too. Josie reassured her that Clark was a godsend. The orchards had been pruned, the winter garden tended, and they would get spring planting done on schedule. Auntie M said she loved the idea that Miles and Josie would work together managing Halstead Farm and Wild Rose.

"You're going to be so happy, honey," she said.

"Thanks, Auntie M. I can't wait to be married to Miles."

Josie called Alex next.

Her older sister thoroughly approved. "The day he brought you home from the hospital, I had a feeling there was something going on between you two."

"Alex, I'd just pushed out a baby. The last thing

on my mind that day was to get something 'going on' with Miles."

"Maybe you were oblivious, but I saw it coming. You and Miles Halstead were meant for each other…"

Josie laughed. "I can't believe you're all in with this."

"Why can't you believe it?"

"I guess I thought you would be more cautious. That you would remind me I needed to carefully weigh the pros and cons. I pictured you warning me that I'm rushing into this, and I ought to slow down."

"Well, okay. Let's try that. Have you carefully weighed the pros and cons of this marriage, Josephine?"

"Maybe not carefully enough…"

"Do you want to back out?"

"No! Of course, I don't."

"Wonderful. Because a good husband is exactly what you need, and Miles is a stand-up guy. You love those girls of his and I'm guessing he's amazing with Davy."

"He is."

"Plus, there's the whole hot-farmer thing he's got going on."

"True. Very, very true…" She stared out the front window, her fingers straying to her lips, reliving the feel of his kiss.

"All that aside, though." Alex's voice had softened. "If you have doubts, you *should* put the brakes on."

Put the brakes on. Her heart grew heavy just at the thought. "No. I do want to marry Miles. And I don't want to wait."

"Well, then. There you go. I was right. You're going to be deliriously happy. Miles is a lucky man."

Josie snort-laughed. "And you know everything before anyone else does."

"Yes, I do. Big sisters always do. And I'm pleased you've finally seen the light on that." Alex offered to help in any way she could.

Josie wanted to reach through the phone and hug her good and hard. "Thank you. And I know you're busy. But we want the wedding to be soon. I'm thinking the Saturday after next."

"Whew. Not wasting any time, are you?"

"No, we're not. And I know you always go into work Saturdays. Clear it with your boss. Miles and I don't want to wait, and I want you here for it."

"I'll be there," Alex promised.

Once she and Alex said goodbye, Josie called Payton.

Payton said, "Wow. Miles Halstead. Should I have known this would happen?"

"I don't see how."

"No, really." Payton drew a slow breath. "Josie, are you sure?"

"I am, yes."

A silence fell between them. Then Payton said softly, with urgency, "I'll come down right away. I should never have left you in the first—"

"Don't go there. I mean it. You did nothing wrong. You married the man you love who just happens to be your sons' father. Your life is in Seattle, and you did exactly the right thing by moving there."

"But you—"

"I am wild over Miles, Payton. He's the definition of a good man. When he takes me in his arms, I forget my own name and I mean that in all the most naughty, wonderful ways. He adores my son and I've always loved Hazel and Ashley. Miles and I want all the same things in life and we're going to have them."

"So you're sure, then?"

"Yes."

"Well. Okay, then. You love the man. It's happened fast, but sometimes love is like that. It's what they always say—when you know, you know. I'm happy for you."

Love. There it was again.

But come on. What had loving a man ever brought her but heartbreak?

Josie didn't need to go there. She knew what

she wanted—a good life with Miles. She would marry her true friend, a man she desperately wanted, a man with whom she had everything in common.

Yes, the love question bothered her a little. But not enough to change how happy she felt at the thought of making a life with Miles. For the thousandth time since that afternoon, she held out her hand, fingers spread, and admired her perfect ring. "Thank you. I'm happy, too."

"And the more I think about it," Payton said, "the less surprised I am. In so many ways, you two are made for each other."

"That's pretty much what Alex said." Josie explained about wanting the wedding to be simple and in the very near future. "It will be small. Just the families. Essentially, we're eloping—only without going anywhere far from home."

Payton suggested, "How about the Heartwood Inn?"

"Wow. You're serious?"

"I am."

The Heartwood Inn was a few miles from Wild Rose, on the outskirts of town. Payton had met Easton there five and a half years before. Now, the inn belonged to the Wright family company, Wright Hospitality. As CEO of the company, Easton had pushed for a large-scale renovation and made it happen.

Josie teased, "Well, I hear the Heartwood Inn is gorgeous now."

"You heard right."

"And the gardens and the river views are breathtaking." Surrounded by thick woods, the inn was right on the river. "Even this early in the season, though, I'm guessing it will be booked up."

"Leave it to me. I'll pull some strings. It will be Easton's and my wedding present to you."

"It's too much."

"I beg your pardon. When it comes to my sisters, it's never too much. Let me talk to Easton and I'll call you back."

An hour later, it was all arranged. Josie and Miles would marry in the wooded garden at Heartwood Inn. Afterward, they would celebrate by sharing dinner with their immediate families in a small private dining room that looked out on the big trees and the lovely grounds.

For their wedding night, the bride, the groom and Davy would stay in the Columbia Suite, which included a luxurious master bedroom and bath, a beautiful central living area with a fully stocked bar, 24-hour room service…and a second bedroom just for Davy.

Josie's eyes blurred with happy tears. "Payton. I really don't know what to say."

"You don't need to say anything. Just be happy."

"I promise you, I will."

* * *

The next twelve days flew by in a whirlwind of wedding preparations.

By some lovely trick of fate, Josie's wedding day dawned clear and a little bit warmer than expected for early April. Even the wind cooperated, blowing mild and cool. At noon, Josie, her sisters, her aunt, Miles's daughters and Donna Halstead all gathered at Heartwood Inn's Wild Ginger Spa.

The adults drank champagne cocktails. For Ashley and Hazel, the spa provided an alcohol-free version made with sparkling water and grapefruit juice. They nibbled delicious croissant sandwiches and got the full spa treatment—hair, nails and makeup.

Donna raised her glass. "To the bride and groom. I could easily become accustomed to luxury like this."

Payton leaned between their spa chairs to tap Donna's glass with hers. "It's a far cry from the Heartwood Inn of old, that's for sure."

"I'll drink to that," agreed Donna. "Did you ever stay here in the old days?"

Payton's slow grin spoke volumes. "As a matter of fact, I did." Josie knew what her sister was thinking. Five and a half years ago, long before the remodel, Payton had spent every night for a week meeting Easton in one of the rustic suites upstairs. The likelihood was very high that her twin sons had been conceived at the inn.

Donna nodded, her grin as wide as Payton's. "Miles Senior and I stayed here for our first anniversary. The walls, the ceiling, the tables, the chairs—all knotty pine. And the beds were made of aspen logs with canopies created of twisting branches."

"And the plaid," added Payton, putting the back of her hand to her forehead, like a Victorian lady sinking to her fainting couch. "We must never forget the plaid…"

"The curtains, the bedding, the chair cushions— all plaid," Donna explained for the benefit of everyone who hadn't visited the inn in earlier days. "Actually, it was charming in its own way."

Payton nodded. "It's strange, but I have to agree with you. I can't help but feel nostalgic when I think of the way it used to be."

Auntie M raised her glass then. "To the bride and the groom and the beautifully redone Heartwood Inn."

They all drank to that.

At four that afternoon, Josie walked down a slate-rock aisle bordered by giant ferns toward Miles, who looked nervous and so handsome in a black suit. Beside him stood the minister from the Heartwood Methodist Church. Because the gathering was so small, the guests stood. They formed a half circle behind the minister and the groom. Hazel held Davy, who was sound asleep.

"You look beautiful," Miles whispered when she reached his side, his blue gaze sweeping over her, from the top of her head to the hem of her long dress of white lace. Her wisp of a veil didn't cover her face, but flowed back over her hair, which the stylist had gently gathered into a low thick cloud of a ponytail woven with boho braids and bound with jeweled bands. Her bouquet consisted of freesia, ranunculus, sweet peas and tulips in colors ranging from pale pink to the most delicate lilac.

"Ashley, Hazel and David, please join us," said the minister. Miles's daughters stepped forward and turned to flank Josie and Miles on either side. Gently, carefully, Hazel passed the sleeping baby to Josie and accepted her bridal bouquet in exchange.

The minister spoke some more, of the new family they were making, a blending of Miles and his daughters with Josie and Davy. He spoke of kindness and respect and the gentle patience of enduring love.

Love, Josie thought, and her heart felt full. Because there were all kinds of love, really. And she did love Miles, she truly did. Maybe it wasn't romantic love. But it was steady, her love for him.

Since her son's birth, she'd come to love him as a true friend.

And now, today, her love had a new dimension. She loved him as her partner in life.

Davy slept on as she passed him carefully to Miles, who handed him into the arms of his new big sister, Ashley.

Miles took Josie's hand and said his vows first. He slipped a platinum band on her finger, a match for her circle of diamonds.

She'd found a similar band for him. "With this ring, I marry you, Miles Halstead," she said when her turn came, and she slipped her ring on his finger. "With this ring, I bind my life to yours."

When the minister said Miles could kiss his bride, Josie's heart seemed to rise, to reach for him. It would be good for them, this marriage. It would make all their lives better, to go forward together.

She sank into her new husband's deep, arousing kiss, losing herself in his arms. At some point, everyone started clapping and cheering.

The minister laughed, a deep, happy sound. "Clearly a match made in heaven," he said.

All the noise woke Davy. He gave a startled cry and then began yowling. Ashley lifted him to her shoulder and rocked him, but he kept crying.

Josie opened her eyes to see Miles gazing down

at her, a soft smile on those kissable lips of his. "Somebody wants his mama."

She lifted up to kiss him one more time, quick and sweet. And then she turned to Ashley, who handed her the squalling little boy.

In the small dining room with the wall of windows looking out on the beautiful grounds, she fed her baby a bottle of her milk. After he ate, there was changing and soothing, both of which Miles volunteered to do so that Josie could sit with the family and enjoy a glass of cold, delicious champagne.

Davy settled down eventually. He slept through the toasts and the wedding dinner. Payton took him when he fussed during the cake cutting. Overall, he did wonderfully, in large part due to Payton's thoughtfulness in providing a small room off their dining room, which had been furnished with a comfortable chair, a small sofa and Davy's travel bassinet for him to nap in.

It was after eight when the party broke up. Ashley and Hazel went home with Donna. Payton, Easton and the twins returned to Payton's cottage on Wild Rose Farm. Marilyn and Ernesto went to her house across from Payton's. And Alex, as usual, got on the road to Portland.

As for Josie, her new husband and baby Davy, they went upstairs to the Columbia Suite.

* * *

Happier than he'd been in a long, long time, Miles waved the keycard in front of the reader and opened the door, then pushed it inward. He flicked on the light to reveal a sleek yet rustic sitting room. The modern gas fireplace had a beautiful slate surround. The adjoining wall was all windows, with a view of the river, and the furniture had been upholstered in soothing neutral colors.

"It's gorgeous," said Josie, stepping inside with the sleeping Davy in her arms.

"The Wright family know what they're doing," Miles agreed.

She went to the window. It was past dark, but outside lights provided a soft glow that showcased the vivid greens of ferns, azaleas and rhododendrons, with the deeper greens of the pines and firs above.

Miles stared at her slim back, at her cloud of amber hair all braided and coiled, her soft, flowing dress of white lace. She looked like a princess in some medieval fairy tale. He felt a deep satisfaction that she belonged to him now, that they would have a life together, work together, share a house and a table.

And at night, his bed.

As though she'd heard him thinking, she sent

him a dewy smile over her shoulder. "Let's tuck this boy into his bassinet."

He went to her. Resting his hands on her pretty shoulders, he nuzzled her hair. "I'll take him."

"There's a baby monitor in the suitcase I brought for him." The Wrights had seen to everything, including having their bags brought up to the suite ahead of time. "The suitcase should be in his room."

"I'll take care of it," he said.

"I know you will." She turned her head back to him and he tasted her lips briefly.

Really, she amazed him. He'd thought he'd found true happiness on the night he married Fiona.

But this.

It was different. Better. He realized he'd never felt completely comfortable around his first wife. There'd always been that edge, a mystery about her that he couldn't breach—a mystery that remained unsolved until she died. A mystery that hid an ugly, unacceptable truth.

But Josie...

Josie was like the sun. Bright, open. Willing to show a man exactly who she was. He hated that any man had ever hurt her.

But if no man had hurt her, he wouldn't be here with her now. If that first boyfriend back in high school had appreciated what he had in her, Miles would never have gotten the chance to put his ring on her finger. He wouldn't have tonight with her.

Or all the nights to come.

He bent to the velvety skin of her neck and pressed his mouth there, sucking a little, using his tongue too, tasting her sweetness.

A low, husky chuckle escaped her. "Miles…"

"Hmm?"

"We need to put the baby to bed."

He didn't want to move from this spot, from this moment, where he had his mouth on her skin, his hands on her shoulders and the scent of her tempting him, making him ache for her. "I need a kiss before I go."

She turned her head back to him again and he claimed her mouth. Nothing had ever tasted as good as she did—Josie, his bride, on their wedding night.

She sighed and their tongues danced together.

And then, in her arms, Davy smacked his lips.

The kiss broke as they focused on the baby.

"Still asleep," she whispered.

"Okay, okay," he said softly in her ear. "I get the message. Hand him over." She turned and passed Davy to him.

He gathered the warm bundle close to his chest, adjusted the blanket around his little face, thought about the years to come, the things he would teach him—to ride a horse, to prune a pear tree, to treat women with respect and look out for those who couldn't take care of themselves.

In the smaller of the two bedrooms, Miles tucked the sleeping baby into the travel bassinet. He set up the baby monitor. Taking the receiver with him, he left the room, shutting the door silently behind him.

Josie wasn't in the living area. The door to the larger bedroom stood open, though. He went to stand in the doorway and found her sitting on the end of the king-size bed, still wearing her white dress.

"There's champagne on ice on the counter in here," he offered. "Shall I open it?"

She looked at him and slowly shook her head. "Come in." She held out her slender hand.

Leaving the monitor on a narrow table by the bedroom door, he moved to stand above her. Holding her gaze, he took off his jacket, tie and white dress shirt, tossing each one across the nearest chair.

"Come up here..." He pulled her to her feet and into his arms.

"Miles..." She ran her hands over his bare chest, her fingers nimble and cool.

They shared a kiss—it was deep and sweet and endless. And then he knelt at her feet. She sat down again, and he eased off her low-heeled lace shoes.

"You're beautiful," he said, wrapping his hands around her ankles, sliding them upward over the sleek skin of her legs, taking the feather-light fabric of her dress along with him, molding the shape of her strong calves, tracing the shadowed curves behind her knees.

She leaned forward as he edged up. They kissed again, slowly. He couldn't get over it. They were actually married now. They had all the damn time in the world to be together, to have each other.

With his fingers, he memorized the bones of her knees, slipping his hands higher, to the smooth, firm skin of her thighs.

He drank a sigh from those lips of hers.

She pulled away to gaze up at him, her eyes shining bright as stars. "Help me with my hair?"

"In a minute…" His hands moved higher. He let them wander outward, to the twin curves of her hips. "A thong."

She giggled. "Ya got me."

He took the little strings of satin in either hand and tugged on them. She lifted. He swept the wisp of nothing down her thighs and off. Twirling the thong on a finger, he let it go somewhere behind him.

She said, "I don't know if I ever told you. I'm on the pill."

He pushed the dress higher. "Good. I have condoms, but without is better. Closer."

"Yeah." She had that breathless sound now. He loved when she sounded like that.

He pushed the skirt of her dress all the way to where her pretty thighs met her body. "Lift up again." When she obeyed, he eased the yards of delicate lace out from under her. "Lie back."

She stretched out on the big bed with the skirt of her dress fanning out beneath her body. He moved in closer between her spread thighs, pushing the froth of lace higher on her belly, until she was bare for him from the waist down. So pretty, smooth and sleek, with only a neat strip of tight curls at the top of her mound.

He lowered his mouth to her. She sighed when he kissed her. Lifting her feet, she braced them on his shoulders. He drank in the soft, pleasured sounds she made as he teased her with his fingers and his tongue. It felt so good, so right, to be with her like this, kissing her, stroking her...

She cried his name as she came.

He stayed with her, right there at her feet, until her breathing evened out.

When she held out her hand to him, he took it and began to rise, pulling her up with him. She kissed him, her lips sweet and open, moving against his own.

He lifted a hand to stroke her braided hair. "So pretty..."

"Take it down, please."

"Now?"

She turned in his arms. "Now."

The process took a while. He eased off the bands and undid each braid until the heavy mass lay thick on her shoulders and down her back.

They undressed quickly and fell together across the bed, holding each other so tight. She was sleek and strong in his arms. He couldn't get enough of kissing her, touching her, memorizing every curve, every secret nook and hollow.

She danced her clever fingers down the center of his chest and wrapped them firmly around his aching erection. Staring into his eyes, her soft lips parted, her breath coming fast and hungry, she began stroking him. It felt so good. He almost lost it.

Just in time, he took charge and rolled her beneath him. She sighed out his name as she opened to him, lifting her legs, wrapping them around him.

White-hot, so sweet. He had no words for how it felt to hold her like this, to be within her and around her. To know she was his and he would be hers for the rest of their lives.

Forget true love and all that hearts-and-flowers garbage.

This—him and Josie, married, together. A union built on honesty, trust, mutual respect and a whole lot of fireworks. He'd thought he would spend the rest of his life alone. Raise his girls, run the farm, get through each day, one after another.

And yet here he was, with Josie soft and pliant in his arms. Here he was, looking forward to tomorrow again, feeling like the luckiest man on the face of the earth.

Because he was lucky. Life had surprised him again, this time in the best way, with a wife who seemed made just for him. And as she shattered beneath him and he let his own finish roll through him, he knew that it would only get better as each day passed.

Deep in the night, Josie heard her baby crying. She opened her eyes to a strange room.

And then she remembered—the wedding. She and Miles were married…

Davy wailed louder.

Next to her, her new husband stirred. He turned on the lamp and then leaned over her, his straight, shiny hair falling over his eyes, his big body touching hers, reminding her of earlier, how good he'd felt, holding her, kissing her, so broad and solid and strong. So very much a man.

"I'll get him." He smiled down at her.

"I can do it." Her breasts ached a little. "He's hungry."

He bent close, dropped a quick kiss on her lips and whispered, "I'll bring him to you."

He rolled away and off the big bed, not a stitch on. She laced her hands behind her head and enjoyed the view as he headed for the door, leaving it open behind him.

A minute later, Davy quieted a little—she assumed because Miles had picked him up. She could hear Miles murmuring to him, saying soothing words she couldn't quite make out.

When Miles reappeared in the doorway cradling the baby against his broad chest, she held out her arms. Miles handed him over along with a burp cloth. Davy rooted around, fussing, making angry little noises, as Miles helped her get comfortable by adjusting the pillows against the headboard behind her. She'd dropped off to sleep wearing nothing, so there were no clothes to undo and no point in covering herself while she nursed. Miles, after all, was her husband now.

Husband. She pondered that word. It hardly seemed possible that she had a husband. Since Taylor Brentwood had left her in the dust and then quickly married someone else, she'd never planned to have a husband. Ever.

Davy latched on and the room was suddenly silent.

Miles got back into the bed. She thought how he looked like just the kind of man she might fantasize about sharing a bed with. It all felt completely natural, to be nursing her baby, naked in bed with an equally naked Miles at her side.

Natural, yet all new. And maybe a little bit unreal—scratch that. A lot unreal.

"I'll take him when he's finished eating," Miles said. He stretched out beside her, punched at the pillow a couple of times, plunked his head down and closed his eyes.

For the next half hour, she nursed her baby on one side and then the other as the feeling of unreality increased. When Davy finished, the man beside her seemed to be sound asleep.

But when she put Davy on her shoulder, Miles opened his eyes. "Finished?"

That sense of unreality vanished just like that.

She gave Miles a big smile. "Yeah." She handed the baby to him and snuggled down in the bed again.

The next time she woke, daylight brightened the edges of the drawn curtains and Miles was still wrapped around her.

He stirred. "Morning." His lips brushed her shoulder. She turned in his arms and they celebrated their brand-new union all over again. It was every bit as good as the lovemaking the night before.

When the baby started fussing, she fed him while Miles ordered them breakfast. As soon as Davy finished, Miles took him, burped him, changed him and held him while they ate.

Really, Miles Halstead had a whole lot going for him, husband-wise.

It was a little after ten when they packed up to go.

They'd arrived in separate vehicles, so they caravanned back to the farms. Miles took the lead. Josie had Davy, of course.

During the drive, she started getting that feeling of unreality again. Every spare moment the past thirteen days had been all about the wedding. They'd never even talked about her moving into Miles's place.

He'd probably just assumed that she would. She supposed she had, too. His house was bigger than hers, and they needed room for all three kids now.

Really, she should have planned for today, should have at least packed what she would require for the immediate future. All her stuff was at her place. She didn't even have enough diapers in Davy's bag to get through tonight.

A weird sense of panic came over her, rising from the pit of her stomach, spreading all through her.

Was any of this real?

Boom! Just like that, she was married. Maybe she really should have slowed things down a little, put the brakes on, given herself more time to be sure that marriage was the right choice.

Yeah, Miles was pretty much everything she'd ever hoped for in a man. But they hadn't been together for that long, really. They'd been friends for a couple of months, shared a few kisses. And then he'd proposed—and she'd said yes.

It had all happened so fast. She'd pretty much jumped in the deep end without a life jacket.

The turnoff to Halstead Farm came up on the left. Miles took it.

Josie kept right on going.

Chapter Eight

Josie pulled her Renegade to a stop in front of her cottage. A glance in the rearview showed her that Davy was sound asleep in his car seat, his head drooping to the side like a heavy flower on a weak stem, his pink lips pooched out, drooling a little.

Her panic receded a bit at the sight of him, her baby boy, dreaming away, all sweet and peaceful, completely oblivious to the emotional havoc going on inside his mama.

Too bad all her anxiety surged back full force when Miles, his tires kicking up dust, pulled to a hard stop behind her. Before she could decide whether to get out and meet him halfway or just wait for him to come to her, he was already knocking on her side window.

She rolled it down. "Um. Hey."

He leaned in the window, bringing the scent of soap and evergreen, reminding her sharply of the glory of last night. "What's up?" he asked, carefully neutral, waiting for her to explain why she'd sped on by the turnoff to his house.

She was sweating, wet under the arms. Her face felt hot. Really, what could she say to him? How could she explain herself? "I realized that all my stuff is here. So I was thinking that I'll just, you know, stay here tonight and we can work it all out later."

There. At least she'd said something, even if it did come out sounding completely ridiculous.

Miles studied her face for an agonizing count of ten. He didn't look happy—not that he should look happy. He'd apparently expected her to go to his place with him and she'd kind of expected she would do that, too.

She had a feeling he was hovering on the verge of demanding that she come home with him now.

But he surprised her. "Okay, then," he said quietly. "I'll see you tomorrow."

"Um. Yeah. Tomorrow. Great."

"One thing, though..."

"Yeah?"

He reached in the window, framed her face

between his big hands and kissed her. When he pulled away, she almost grabbed him back. "Tomorrow," he said and turned for his pickup.

She watched him in her sideview mirror as he got back behind the wheel. A moment later, he swung his pickup around her Jeep. She watched him circle the driveway that ran between the cottages. In no time at all, he disappeared down the access road, headed back toward his place.

As soon as his truck vanished from sight, Auntie M and Payton emerged from their separate cottages. Josie had barely gotten out of the Jeep before they descended on her.

"What happened?" demanded Payton.

"Sweetheart, are you okay?" cried Auntie M.

No, she was not. She had no idea why she hadn't just followed Miles home—or at least, expressed her weird inner confusion just now when he'd asked her what was going on.

But she hadn't done either.

And right now, she just wanted to get Davy and all his gear and her suitcase into the house. She wanted to brew herself some tea and sit at her kitchen table and stare out the nearest window for a while.

"I'm fine," she said. "I promise you."

"But you don't *seem* fine," argued Payton.

"Shouldn't you be with Miles?" asked Marilyn.

Payton's frown deepened. "Did something go wrong between you two?"

"Nothing went wrong," Josie insisted. Auntie M and Payton just stood there. They looked at her with similar expressions of concern. She tried again. "Everything's okay."

"Oh, honey," her aunt cried, reaching for her.

Josie found herself wrapped in her aunt's loving arms. Payton joined them and they shared a three-way hug.

"Don't worry," she said when they finally let her go. "I mean it. I'm great. Terrific." Was she trying too hard? Yep. She dialed it back. "It was a beautiful wedding, the wedding of my dreams. The suite was amazing. Miles and I had the perfect wedding night."

"You did?" Payton grabbed her by the shoulders and looked deeply into her eyes. "Truly?"

"Truly. It was wonderful. All is well." Honestly, how many ways could she say she was fine? "And right now, I need to take my baby and my things inside and go check on the pear orchard."

No, the pear orchard did not need checking on. But she was running out of ways to say she didn't want to talk right now.

And it worked—or maybe Payton and her aunt finally got the message that she just needed a little time alone. They pitched in to carry everything into the cottage and then stayed to look after Davy so that she could go out to the orchard, as she'd insisted she needed to do.

The walk out there did kind of help. She strode between the rows of budding trees, the wind whipping her spiral curls around her head, and felt better, being home on Wild Rose Farm.

The center of calm she'd found in the orchard persisted when she returned to the cottage, where Payton had remained to keep an eye on Davy until she returned.

Payton said, "Dinner at Auntie M's. Six o'clock."

"I'll be there," Josie promised.

"Auntie M will be here for a week."

"I know that."

"Easton, the boys and I were planning on staying until Tuesday," Payton said in an offhand way. As if Josie didn't know that, too.

"What are you getting at?"

"Well. I can stay longer if you—"

"Payton."

"Hmm?" All casual and cool.

"Thank you. I love you. Go home with your family as planned. We will be fine here."

Payton didn't ask "Are you sure?" But Josie could see the question lurking in her eyes. "All righty. See you at six."

Josie spent the rest of the day doing nothing in particular. She cuddled Davy. straightened up the cottage and baked a couple of pies to use up the last of the fruit she'd frozen last fall. She took one of them to dinner at her aunt's, where everyone kindly avoided the elephant in the room. The twins were adorable, and no one asked why she was here, while her groom was at the farm next door.

Auntie M followed her out to the porch when she left. "Ernesto has to go back to California next Saturday," she began.

"I've been through this with Payton already. No, you are not staying behind. Go with Ernesto—if he needs to leave earlier, go with him. I mean it. I'm doing great here."

Her aunt wrapped her big sweater a little tighter around her. "You just got married. Your husband's not here. You are not doing great and I'm only letting you know that I'll be staying until you work out whatever's going on between you and Miles."

Josie had Davy in a portable baby seat. She adjusted the blankets a bit around his face and straightened his warm ribbed cap. "Auntie M, you're so obstinate," she muttered through clenched teeth.

"Maybe that's where you get it from."

"Har-har."

"I mean it, Josephine. I'm not leaving you here like this. You need to talk to me or to Payton—

or better yet, work out whatever the problem is with Miles."

"There is no problem." And there wasn't. Not really. She'd just had a weird moment there this morning when he'd turned off for Halstead Farm…and she'd kept going straight, toward the only home she'd ever known. Now she felt like a fool—a fool who had no idea what to do next. "I just need a little time, okay? It all happened so fast, and I need time to catch up emotionally."

"Did Miles do something to upset you?"

"No. He's been nothing but absolutely wonderful. As a matter of fact, I'm wild for that man." *Maybe too wild. Maybe wilder than I ever intended to be.*

"Wild for your husband." Auntie M stepped closer. She kissed Josie's cheek and whispered, "What a terrible thing."

"Don't make fun of me."

"Never." Auntie M guided a stray coil of hair off Josie's cheek. "Go to him. Talk to him. You'll work it out."

Josie knew her aunt was right. "I will. Tomorrow."

Auntie M kissed her cheek again and stood on the porch until Josie crossed the slope of lawn and mounted the steps to her place.

In the cottage, Josie nursed her baby and put him to bed in his own room, lingering for a while, thinking of all Miles had done to fix up this room—the gorgeous reclaimed-wood shelves, the paint job. He'd made that cubby cabinet for Davy's future toys, too, and painted it a cheery red. It looked great against the wall that faced the changing table.

He'd been so good to her in so many ways. And she had no idea what she would say to him tomorrow.

She put on her pajamas, brushed her teeth and then ended up on the sofa for hours watching back-to-back episodes of *Schitt's Creek*, avoiding the loneliness of her own bed.

When she finally did go to bed, she couldn't sleep. She wished for strong arms around her, a warm, solid chest at her back.

Morning came too soon. She woke to Davy's fussy cries from the other room. It was barely daylight, and she felt every bit as cranky as her baby sounded.

"Coming, I'm coming..." she muttered to herself as she dragged her tired body from bed.

The doorbell rang just as she took him from the bassinet. He cried harder as she headed for the main room. Figuring it had to be Payton, come to see how she was doing under the pretense of inviting her for breakfast, she started talking as she opened the door. "I'm fine and you don't need to..."

"Good morning," said Miles.

She blinked up at him, thinking how great he looked, in jeans and a cream-colored waffle-weave Henley with the long sleeves pushed up to reveal those strong forearms of his. "Uh, morning."

He gestured at the pickup behind him. It had a double horse trailer hitched to the back. "I brought a big trailer. Boxes and tape, too. I'm hoping to get you moved in today, if possible. You got chores you need handled?"

"No." Davy cried even louder. She rocked him from side to side. "Clark will take care of it."

"Here. Let me have him." He held out those fine arms. She handed Davy over and he quieted instantly. For a slow count of three, the baby stared up at Miles. Then his face scrunched up again and he let out a yowl.

"He's hungry," she said, her heart going a mile a minute, thinking that she'd never been so happy to see anyone in her whole life. All night, she'd stewed over what to say to him this morning, and he just showed up with a trailer and boxes to pack up her stuff, telling her without actual words everything she needed to know—that he really did want her with him, in his house. In his bed.

Miles understood her. And he'd chosen exactly the right way to show her that he did. She'd married a wonderful, thoughtful, perceptive man.

Yeah, the love thing nagged at her. Sometimes lately, she felt so deeply for him. Sometimes she couldn't help thinking that the more she knew him, the more she would care for him. Until it was no longer possible to call what she felt anything but the one word they'd agreed they wouldn't use with each other.

What a silly, bitter fool she'd been, to have ever tried to tell herself that she was done with love. No person was ever done with love. Even with a heart broken beyond repair, the yearning for that special connection with at least one other human being could never really die.

But this morning, with him standing in the doorway, her crying baby cradled in his arms, she at least knew that she'd made the right choice to marry him. She knew that he wanted a life with her the same as she wanted to be with him.

They could take it day-to-day.

Miles grinned...or maybe it was more of a grimace. "He smells like it might be time for a diaper change."

"No kidding—the girls?"

"They stayed at my mother's last night. They'll be back home after school today." At her nod, he said, "And Josie..."

"Yeah?"

His grin faded as he held her gaze. "We should have talked about it, about your coming home with me. I just assumed that you would want what I want. That was wrong. Josie, I want you with me. I want my house to be our house."

"I want that, too," she said as Davy cried louder.

"Good." He bent over Davy and whispered, "Shh, little man. It's all going to work out, you'll see." Then he looked up at her again. "How about you make me some coffee while I change him— then you can feed him?"

"Deal." She ushered her new husband inside.

She and Miles had just finished breakfast when Payton showed up. As soon as Josie's sister learned that it was moving day, she went to get Easton, Auntie M and Ernesto to help out. Even the four-year-old twins pitched in. Working together, they loaded Miles's pickup, the horse trailer and Josie's Jeep with all the things Josie didn't want to do without, including everything in Davy's room, from the new crib to the reclaimed wood shelves.

"Too bad my farm mural isn't packable." Josie felt a twinge of sadness that she couldn't take it, too.

Miles set down the toy cabinet he'd built and came to take her in his arms. "You can stencil one in his new room." He kissed the end of her nose.

She lifted her mouth and he captured her lips.

"Newlyweds," muttered Ernesto in a teasing

tone as he tried to edge around them with a big box full of baby gear. Josie and Miles broke apart, laughing. "Get back to work, you two." Ernesto faked a stern expression. "All this stuff won't load itself, you know." He muttered something in Italian as he went out.

Miles felt good—damn good. He and Josie were back on track and her family had joined right in to help her move.

Yesterday had been tough. He wanted Josie with him, but he'd had the feeling that making a big deal of her sudden decision to spend the night at her cottage would not go down well.

So he'd let her go and then spent a sleepless night wondering if their marriage was over before it had really begun. This morning, when he hooked up the horse trailer, he'd had no clue if the approach he'd chosen would work...or blow up in his face. But a little while later, when she opened her door to him and he watched her eyes light up at the sight of him, he finally let himself breathe a long, slow sigh of relief.

By three thirty that afternoon, his garage was stacked high with full boxes *and* the guest-room furniture from the downstairs back bedroom, which had now become Davy's room.

"I think we're pretty much set for now," Josie

told her sister when Payton asked what else they needed to bring from the other house.

"Want to come on back to Wild Rose?" asked Marilyn. "Eat with us?"

Josie sent Miles a questioning glance, and then before he could say a word, she made up her own mind. "The girls will be home soon. I think we'll fix something here."

"First family dinner," said Marilyn with a smile. "I get it. Sounds good."

"I'll be over tomorrow to say goodbye," Josie promised her sister.

Miles offered, "I'll drive you guys back."

"No need," said Easton, taking the hands of each of his sons. "It's a short walk and a beautiful day."

Miles put his arm around Josie. She leaned into him. He brushed a kiss against her temple as they stood together at the end of the driveway, Bruce and Tink on either side of them, to watch the others go.

Half an hour later, Hazel and Ashley arrived home. Miles considered it a lucky accident of fate that they'd stayed in town Sunday night. Teenage daughters could be completely oblivious, but no way would they have failed to notice that Josie hadn't come home from the inn with him. He had no clue how he might have explained his new bride's absence to them. Thankfully, he didn't have to.

The girls climbed from the VW and went straight to Josie for happy hugs of greeting.

Hazel brought in her small suitcase and then hurried off to the rescue barn at Wild Rose, promising to be back within the hour.

Ashley, as always, started working on him to let her return to town. "I left my chem notebook at Rory's," she said. "I need to go get it. And Darlene invited me to stay for dinner. I'll be back by ten at the latest."

He tamped down his irritation. She'd just arrived home and, as always lately, she couldn't wait to be gone again. "Not tonight, Ash. It's a family night."

"Dad." Her voice had turned wheedling. "You don't need me here."

"I want you here. We all do."

"But I need my notebook."

"Ask Aurora to bring it to school tomorrow."

"I need it...and okay, fine. Nine. I'll be back at—"

"Ashley, I want you to stay home with us tonight."

"I don't believe this. Eight, then?"

"No."

"But—"

"No."

She glared and fumed, but at least she quit trying to manipulate him. "Fine." Spinning on her heel, she stormed up the stairs, no doubt headed for her room. He stared after her, wincing when her door slammed shut.

A moment later, Josie's arms came around him from behind. Laying his hands over her smaller ones, feeling the warmth of her at his back, he relaxed. Nobody ever said parenting was easy. And he could really get used to being married to this woman.

"Shall I go talk to her?" his wife asked.

"No." He turned, put a finger under her pretty chin and tipped her face up to brush a quick kiss across her lips. "Let her cool off a little. She'll be fine."

An hour later, when they all sat down to eat, Ashley was wearing a scowl. But Hazel chattered away about that special kitten she wanted to adopt and an art project she and two other girls were putting together at school. Josie asked Ash how Aurora and her family were doing. Ashley launched right into a story about the new deck cover Rory's dad and uncle were building. After that, Ash's mood slowly lightened. At least she talked to Josie and Hazel. By the time they got up to clear the table, Ash seemed to have left the sulking behind.

And when Davy's cries started in from the back bedroom, she jumped up to go get him before Hazel did.

"You need me, you call me." Payton's hands settled on Josie's shoulders. "I'll be here." They stood on the porch at Payton's cottage. The boys and Easton were already in the car. "I mean that."

"I know you do. And don't worry. Yeah, I had a minor freak-out there on Sunday, but everything's great now. Miles and I are solid."

"Solid." Payton peered at her as though trying to read her mind.

Josie tried again. "We're good. Happy."

That answer seemed to satisfy Payton. She nodded. "I'm glad, and I'll be back on Friday, the sixth."

"Did you think I'd forgotten?" Josie asked in a teasing tone. They'd agreed months ago that Payton would come to help out on the first Heartwood Saturday Market of the season.

"Of course not. I'm just, you know, confirming."

Josie laughed. "How many ways can I tell you I'm happy and all is well?"

"Just reach out, okay? Anytime."

"You know I will."

Auntie M stepped up next. She handed Davy to Josie and hugged Payton goodbye.

Once Payton and the boys drove off, Josie offered to help her aunt pack. Marilyn and Ernesto were moving more of her things down to Salinas. But Auntie M said she and Ernesto had the rest of the week to fill the U-Haul they'd rented. They weren't leaving until Saturday.

Josie checked on Clark, who had everything under control, as usual. She invited him to dinner at Halstead Farm and he said he would be there.

With Davy comfy in his sling and Tink nearby, she gathered eggs and transplanted the broccoli seedlings she'd started hardening off a week and a half before. It felt good to dig in the dirt a bit.

That night at her new home with Miles, they had both Clark and Rafe over for dinner. After the meal, all four of them—Miles, Josie and the two hands—adjourned to the office Miles had created from a section of the back porch. They agreed on how they would all work together to run both farms, and they started dividing up the chores to make that happen. Josie would not only be handling Heartwood Saturday Market, but she would also run the new joint farm stand, too.

Miles asked when she was expected to go back on-call for Heartwood Animal Clinic. When she said June, he asked how they were managing to hold her spot for her.

"Old Dr. Meuller is taking my place until I

come back." Doc Meuller had retired a few years before.

"You want to go back sooner?" Miles asked. "We can shuffle things around any time you get a call. I'm not bad at the market and they love me at the farm stand."

"I have no doubt." Still, she shook her head. "I want the time with Davy while he's so little. But if Doc Meuller stops being available, yes. I'll go back early."

"No problem," said Miles. "We'll make it work."

She already knew that they would. Miles was a cooperative, helpful man. Still, it felt good to have him say it. Before they'd decided to get married, she'd spent more than one sleepless night stewing over how she would manage both the farm and the career she'd worked so hard for.

Their marriage made everything a little easier for her. *Miles* made everything a little easier for her—easier, happier, better in every way.

She only wished she didn't miss Payton and the twins so much. Her sister hadn't even been gone a whole day and Josie already felt a sort of empty space in her heart.

"You're quiet tonight," Miles said later, when it was just the two of them alone in the bed where she'd given birth to Davy.

She turned into him and snuggled closer. He shifted to slip an arm around her.

"It's not a big deal," she said. "But I do feel a little sad…"

He got hold of a coil of her hair and started wrapping it around a finger. "Sad because…?"

"It's nothing, really."

Miles tugged on the curl of hair he'd been fiddling with. "Talk to me."

"Well, everything's changing, that's all. Auntie M is essentially moving to Salinas to be with Ernesto. I'm here with you. Payton's up in Seattle. Except for Clark, nobody will be living full-time on Wild Rose."

"And that makes you sad?"

"Hmm." Was *sad* the right word? "Wistful, maybe. It's like the end of an era."

"But Payton and your aunt will be coming back all the time. And they'll be staying in their cottages when they do."

"True. They love Wild Rose as much as I do. It's not like I'll never see them. It's just different than it used to be, that's all."

"You know, you said pretty much the same thing back in February, when I dropped by to check on you after they all left." He skated a finger down the slope of her nose.

She busted herself. "I did, didn't I?"

"It's going to work out well, you'll see." He

traced the shell of her ear, a slow, light caress. His touch felt so good.

"You mean with us working together to run both farms?"

"Yeah."

"I agree." She returned his smile, her melancholy mood eased by his patience and tenderness.

He kissed her cheek and let his lips trail down to the tip of her chin. "Another thing I'm really happy about..."

"Counting our blessings, are we?"

"Absolutely. I like having you here in my bed every night. I like it a lot. I'm looking forward to years of this, a whole lifetime's worth."

"Mmm... Me, too." She ran her palm upward along the outside of his arm from his wrist to his shoulder, stirring the silky brown hairs, loving the strength in him and the feel of work-hardened muscles beneath his warm skin.

He slipped a finger under the lace strap of her sleep cami and slowly guided it down her shoulder until her breast got free. Gently he cupped the soft globe in his palm. Her breath caught as he rubbed her nipple with his thumb and whispered, "So pretty..."

She lifted her mouth to him. He took it. She hooked a leg over his body, pulling him closer, deepening the kiss, her melancholy forgotten as she gave herself up to his kiss.

* * *

Josie had Auntie M and Ernesto over for dinner on Wednesday night. She invited Donna Halstead, too. Miles's mom and Marilyn had gone to Heartwood High together. They'd grown to know each other better when Donna married Miles Sr., and moved to Halstead Farm.

Both of them told great stories of working frantically together to protect the orchards during a sudden late freeze, of a forest fire that swept past every fire line and right into Heartwood, taking out several homes and businesses before the brave firefighters beat it back. The evening went well. Sometimes Miles seemed a little annoyed with his mother, but Josie felt grateful to have a generous, funny, good-hearted mother-in-law like Donna.

Thursday, Josie visited her aunt at Marilyn's cottage. Ernesto had driven over to Heartwood Hardware, so it was just the two of them, Auntie M and Josie, packing up odds and ends in the kitchen. In Salinas, Ernesto owned a big, fully furnished house with a chef-worthy kitchen. Auntie M wouldn't need any of her own cookware or gadgets there. But some things, she wanted with her. They packed those.

When Davy fell asleep, Josie put him in the soft-sided playpen Marilyn had bought when Payton's twins were babies. While he slept, they brewed tea and took it out to sit on the porch together, to sip and chat and enjoy the sunny day.

They spoke of Uncle John Dunham, and how his sudden death had hit Aunt Marilyn hard.

"After John died," Auntie M said of her husband, whom Josie barely remembered, "I thought I was finished with love. The idea of meeting someone new, of falling in love all over again—I didn't want it. I'd loved John so much and I decided that was it for me. I spent years cutting myself off from the happiness a woman has when she finds the right one for her."

Josie leaned her head on her aunt's slim shoulder. "But then along came Ernesto."

Auntie M gave Josie's knee a playful slap. "Don't mock love."

"No, ma'am." Josie faked contrition and a phony Southern accent. "Ah would nevah..."

"You always had that smart-aleck side, now, didn't you?"

"Maybe. A little." Tink was lying with her head on Josie's thigh. Josie scratched her thick ruff. "But go on. About Ernesto..."

Auntie M stared across the slope of lawn toward Payton's cottage, where wild Nootka and wood roses grew on either side of the steps leading up to the porch. The canes were greening up nicely, though the delicate pink flowers wouldn't show their faces until later in the season. "I love

Ernesto," said Auntie M—and she didn't stop there. "With Ernesto, it's as though the whole world has opened up for me. I'm fully alive again at last."

Now Marilyn was the one leaning her head on Josie's shoulder. She went on kind of dreamily. "It's selfish, how grateful I was that your mother had a wild streak and never wanted to stick around much, that I got to raise you and Alex and Payton. You three became all the happiness I let myself have for a quarter of a century. And it was a lot, the joy of being your Auntie M. But still, a big part of my heart stayed shut down for too many years."

Shut down. Josie got that. She'd done the same, really. Not out of grief at the loss of a husband, like Aunt Marilyn. But out of exhaustion from trying to make love work and inevitably finding nothing but disappointment each time she put her heart out there.

"The years go by if you don't take a chance," said Auntie M. "They crawl by…and yet, you look back and realize you've let two and a half decades slip away without that special guy whose hand fits just right in yours."

Josie couldn't quite let that stand. "But you didn't *waste* those years. Come on, Auntie M. You know you didn't. You didn't even know Ernesto until last fall."

Auntie M stroked a hand down Josie's hair.

"Sweetheart, yes I did. Ernesto and Tom Huckston have been friends forever. They met as children here in Heartwood. Tom's father knew Ernesto's father. Then Ernesto and Tom became close friends when they both went to UC Davis way back in the day."

"Yeah, but you didn't really *know* Ernesto in all that time."

"I knew him well enough." Auntie M slanted her a sly look. "Honey, after John died, Ernesto asked me out every time he came to stay at the Huckston farm—well, aside from during the ten years he was married."

"I didn't know he was married."

"Yeah. It didn't last, but he speaks of her fondly. A nice woman from Watsonville." Like Marilyn, Ernesto had no children of his own. "After John died and during the years Ernesto was single, he must have asked me out ten times. I would always say no. It hurt so much when I lost John. I locked my heart away, tried to keep it safe. Now, I just wish I'd been braver sooner. We lost a lot of years that we might have been together, Ernesto and me, because I just wouldn't take a second chance on love."

Auntie M turned her fondest smile on Josie. "That's why I'm so happy that both you and Payton have found what matters most, that you've taken the biggest risk and opened your hearts up to love and commitment."

The ache in Josie's belly twisted deeper. As Auntie M praised her supposed courage to take yet another chance on love, Josie felt like a fake, pure and simple. Right then, she couldn't help but see her marriage not as the happy, practical, safe arrangement she and Miles had agreed on, but as nothing more than a sham.

And Marilyn didn't stop there. "I just want you to know how proud I am of you. I know you've had more than one crippling disappointment in love. But you never gave up. You kept on trying. When the right man didn't come along, you had Davy, anyway. And now, you've found Miles.

"Now, you have everything that really matters. You have true love and a whole new, beautiful family. You're an example to me, Josie. You prove what I wish I'd figured out when I was your age. That a woman can rise above her wounded heart and reach out for love and happiness with both hands."

Josie leaned her head on her aunt's shoulder again—all the better not to meet Marilyn's eyes and possibly give away the turmoil that churned within her.

Because what was she, really? She'd said yes to Miles to make a family, to gain a life companion without risking all the scary, messy crap that can happen when a woman gives her heart. She hadn't been brave or strong. She wasn't an example for anyone.

She'd just taken the easy way out.

Chapter Nine

It got worse.

In the coming days, Josie looked deeper. She watched Miles more closely, took careful inventory of her own interactions with him.

What she discovered taught her more than she'd wanted to know.

Three nights after Marilyn and Ernesto left for Salinas again, Josie and Miles spent hours in a muddy pen at Halstead Farm helping a heifer deliver a breech-birth calf in the pouring rain. When Josie finally pulled out that baby, she fell flat on her back in the mud, with the bawling calf on top of her.

"Are you hurt?" he demanded as he pulled the baby off her.

She groaned, "Never better," and watched as he dragged the bleating little guy several feet away for his mama to deal with.

He came right back to where she was lying, spread-eagled in the mud, the rain pouring down on her as she watched the newborn calf struggle to his feet. The umbilical cord had already broken off by itself at the ideal place a few inches from the little guy's navel, so nothing to worry about on that score. It was just possible that their work here was done. "I will never get up," she announced. "I might just have to lie here in the rain forever."

Miles dropped to his knees beside her and offered his hand. "Josie Halstead, no you won't. You're not a woman who gives up."

"Easy for you to say."

"Because it's true," he replied, his voice a little gruff now. "You've got more heart than any woman I ever knew—now give me your hand."

She put her muddy, bloodied fingers in his and then couldn't resist giving a tug, catching him just at the second when he was unbalanced enough to fall over.

They both grunted as he landed right on top of her. Burying his nose against her neck, he grumbled, "Now that was just mean."

And then they both started laughing. The calf

bleated and the heifer stared at them, the wisdom of the ages in her bulging brown eyes.

"Even though I don't want to get up," she said when she finally stopped laughing, "I was just thinking that our work here is done."

He braced up on his forearms and grinned down at her. "We're farmers. Our work is never done."

"You have a valid point. And we really should get inside." They'd left Hazel with the baby monitor in case Davy woke up.

Miles brushed at her forehead with his muddy hand. "You've got grass in your hair."

"Right now, stuff in my hair is the least of my problems. Get off me, you're heavy."

"You pulled me down here..." His face changed. She knew that look. "You've got the biggest eyes. And those freckles, they get to me..."

She fake-gagged. "I can't believe this. I'm covered in mud and blood and amniotic fluid, and you think you're going to kiss me?"

"Josephine, I don't just think it." His lips touched hers.

And suddenly, he didn't feel heavy at all. She twined her muddy arms around his neck and offered up her mouth to him.

They didn't head for the house until several minutes later. Both dogs trailed along behind them. At least Tink and Bruce had stayed out of the mud for the most part, though their coats were soaked through.

In the garage, they raided a basket of old towels to dry off the dogs and wipe the worst of the mud and other fluids off each other. As they dried the dogs, they laughed together over how Rafe and Clark both disapproved of the way they "spoiled" two good working dogs, coddling them, treating them like fur babies, letting them sleep inside.

Leaving their dirty boots behind, they dropped off the soiled towels in the utility room, sent the dogs to their beds and then tiptoed to Davy's room, where the door was open.

The baby was fast asleep. Carefully, Miles pulled the door shut.

"We should get the monitor from Hazel's room," she said. They had a second receiver in their room, but now there was no need for all of them to wake up if Davy started crying.

Miles hooked his hand around the back of her neck under the muddy mess of her hair and brought that beautiful mouth of his crashing down on hers again.

She wanted to kiss him forever. But after a long, delicious few minutes of tangling tongues and nipping teeth, she pressed her hands against his still-muddy shirt. "I need a shower. Now."

"Go ahead." He swooped down for one more quick, hard kiss. "I'll get the receiver."

Five minutes later, she stood naked under the rain showerhead in their bathroom, reveling in the sheer heaven of washing off all the grime. She heard the clink of a belt buckle. With her face still tipped up to the water, she asked, "Is Hazel asleep?"

"Out like a light."

"Good."

A moment later, she heard the shower door open. Big hands clasped her waist. "Share," he said in a low rumble.

They stood under the sweet rain of clean, hot water, his muscular front to her back. "Feels so good," she said.

He made a sound that was more of a growl than a word. A bolt of pure lust weakened her knees as she felt his hardness against her bottom. And then he was turning her to face him.

She groaned as he kissed her, and whispered, "Yes," when he lifted her and braced her with her back against the wall. She wrapped her legs around him, levering up a little, enough to get him positioned where she needed him. Slowly, she sank down, taking him in.

Nothing had ever felt so perfect in her whole life.

They wasted some water, but it was worth it.

And it wasn't until later, in silence and satisfaction, as Miles slept beside her not long before dawn, that she rolled to her side and stared at his face through the darkness.

Auntie M had pried the lid loose on all her denials. All it took after that was a few days of stewing over the lie she'd been telling herself. A few days of paying very close attention to the man she'd married, to the life they shared.

To his goodness, his gentle ways, his skills as a farmer, his willingness to work, his love for his children, his dry sense of humor. The way he was with Davy. The way her heart sometimes felt like it wanted to push right out of her chest and get closer to his when he held her.

She was her own twist on that old poem by Elizabeth Barrett Browning, the one she'd studied in English class way back in high school, the one that started out "How do I love thee? Let me count the ways..."

How could she possibly count all the ways she admired Miles, respected him, cared for him?

Wanted him...

Gently, so as not to wake him, she brushed a straight hank of hair back off his forehead.

Really, how long had this been going on?

How had her heart changed inside her own chest, from mere liking to real affection, to love, strong and true? How long had she been lying to herself, minimizing the enormity of what she felt for him?

"Oh, Miles…" She whispered the words so as not to wake him. "I'm such a liar…"

So much for safe and convenient and practical. She didn't feel safe. Not anymore.

She loved him. Deeply. Completely. He was her man and there was no one else for her. Love was the real reason she'd said yes when he'd proposed, though she'd refused to admit it to herself at the time.

Poor, wonderful man. She smiled at him sadly through the gloom.

Miles thought she was safe.

Wrong.

She loved him and she wanted him to love her in return, though he'd made it all too clear that he wouldn't.

Or maybe he couldn't…

And what did it matter, couldn't or wouldn't? After Fiona's faithlessness, he would never take another chance on giving his heart.

Get over it, Josephine.

Really, there was no problem here. Yeah, okay. She was something of a coward, one who'd been lying to herself about the love in her own heart.

But so what?

Miles wanted her. He *liked* her. He thought the world of her, and he'd said so more than once. There was absolutely no reason not to just love him in silence and find her fulfillment in the good life they had together.

He had a true heart. He would never do anything to hurt her. In all the ways that mattered most, Miles Halstead was hers.

On the last Tuesday in April, Ashley stayed an extra hour at school to work on a special project. Miles drove into town to pick up Hazel from middle school.

"It's today," Hazel announced as she climbed in on the passenger side and hooked up her seat belt. She flashed him a wide smile, so happy right then that she forgot to be self-conscious about her braces.

"I remember," he replied.

"Take me to the pet store."

He put the car in gear and off they went to buy everything Hazel's new kitten would need. On the drive home, they continued past the turnoff to Halstead Farm. He stopped the pickup in front of Josie's rescue barn.

Hazel went in and came out carrying a fluffy little calico kitten.

At home, in a corner of the utility room off the garage, they set up a kitty station, with food, water, a scratching post and a litter box. The kitten went straight to the box when Hazel let her out of the new carrier.

A few minutes later, as Hazel's pet tucked into her dinner, Ash and Josie appeared in the open doorway.

"She's so pretty," said Ashley. "Have you named her yet?"

"Miss Edith," Hazel replied.

Ash frowned. "You're naming her after your first grade teacher?"

"Yes, I am."

"Why?"

"I really liked Miss Edith. She was strict but fair. She had red hair and glasses with thick black frames and very pale skin. And she moved away to Ashland right before the end of the school year and I missed her. So now I have my own Miss Edith right here with me at home."

"Well, all right, then," said Ash with a slow nod.

Miles caught Josie's eye. They grinned at each other. Too soon, Josie's gaze slid away. He asked Hazel, "So what about the rest of the kittens?"

Hazel scratched Miss Edith between the ears. "Josie already found homes for two of them. I'm going to put up flyers at school for the other two. And there's a volunteer at Heartwood Humane who wants the mama."

"Good news." He glanced at Josie again. He liked that feeling when their eyes met. They had a definite connection, real and solid. Down-to-earth. Marrying her was the smartest thing he'd ever done. She was a true partner, his best friend...with benefits.

And those benefits were nothing short of stellar.

Josie flashed him another smile, one that lit him up inside...until she quickly glanced away again. For half a second or so, he wondered if something was bothering her.

But then she said brightly, "Okay, you guys. Let's get dinner on." She sounded good. Happy. Clearly nothing was bothering her. He followed his daughters and his wife to the kitchen, where he washed his hands and then mashed the potatoes.

After the meal, Ashley, as usual, wanted to drive into town. He got her agreement to return home by nine and then gave the okay. Hazel took Miss Edith upstairs to keep her company while she did her homework.

In the back-porch office, where they each had a desk, Miles and Josie spent some time updating the books for both farms. They paid bills, dealt with online orders and generated invoices. As they worked, they passed Davy back and forth until he dropped off to sleep and Josie put him to bed.

Just an ordinary night with his family. Miles loved every minute of it. And it got better when Ashley came home on time with a smile on her face. Lately, Ash seemed happier, more willing to pitch in around the farm, less ready to fight every challenge to her freedom.

In the last couple of years, Miles had done a lot of worrying about his older daughter. He'd brooded over what she might get up to when she wasn't safe at home. He worried about drugs, about sex, about all the things that could screw up her life before she had the maturity to make good choices—or he *used* to worry.

Not as much recently.

Was it Josie who had made the difference? It kind of seemed so. Ashley had always liked and trusted Josie. Now, with zero resistance or resentment that Miles could see, Ash had happily accepted Josie's new place in the family.

Kids, he thought as he turned out the lights in the great room. Getting them safely to adulthood kept a man up at night and made his hair go gray too soon.

The door to the front bedroom stood open. His wife, her face freshly scrubbed, her hair corralled in a fat ponytail down her back, sat up in bed with a book in her lap. He leaned in the doorway, watching her, thinking how right she looked in his bed.

Eventually, she glanced up. "What?"

"Good book?"

"Oh, yeah. Payton's latest." Josie's sister was a successful author. Payton wrote those sword-and-sorcery books, the kind with dragons and wizards, stories that took place in mythological kingdoms. "It came out last year and I'm just now getting to it. I want to let her know how fabulous I think it is when she comes down next week to help us with Saturday market."

He entered the room. "You're a good sister."

"Thank you. It's not difficult, though, to be a good sister to Payton and Alex. If I need them, they come running. I try to do the same for them." She marked her place and set the book on the nightstand by the lamp.

He locked the door and started shucking off his clothes.

She gave a low laugh. "You've got that look."

"It's all your fault." He tossed his shirt on the nearest chair, dropped his trousers and yanked off his socks. "I don't know what you do to me."

"You're welcome." Amber eyes glowing, she watched him come to her.

He had her little gray pajama shorts and skimpy sleep top off in seconds flat. And then, for an hour, he put everything from his mind but the perfect feel of her in his arms.

Later, when they were lying all wrapped up together in the soft light of her bedside lamp, he couldn't keep his mouth shut. He needed her to know how much she'd come to mean to him.

"This is good," he said, "you and me..."

"Yes, it is." She tipped up her head and kissed his chin. And then she snuggled right back down again.

He nuzzled her hair. "It's better than I ever imagined. Hazel's happy. Since the wedding, Ashley's given me almost no grief. And as for Davy, well, the truth is, I always wanted a boy, too. And now I get to help raise him. And then there's you…"

She tipped back her head again, a hint of a smile on those lips he couldn't get enough of. "Hmm?"

"I can't believe you've lived next door to me all these years and I never knew what I could have with you. I'm just so damn grateful you knocked on my door when Davy came. And I'm grateful you said yes when I popped the question, Josie. I need you to know that I'm happy. So happy. With you."

She gazed up at him, her lower lip quivering a little. Was she going to cry? He was just about to ask her what was wrong when she said, "I, um, guess it wouldn't be the worst thing in the world if we, you know, fell in love…"

Josie wanted to yank the words back as soon as she said them.

Something bad had happened in his eyes—a retreat. A shutting-down.

Okay, she knew they had an agreement. They weren't going to call this thing they had together love. But come on. Hadn't he just essentially said that he loved her? Hadn't he just given her hope that he'd seen the light about what was really going on between them? Hadn't he finally realized that he could trust her enough to let himself say those three little words to her?

For a minute or two, everything had seemed so beautiful, so exactly right.

And now…this.

As she tried to decide what her next words should be, he said, "We agreed. Josie, what we have is so good. But you know I don't believe in all that hearts-and-flowers crap. Never again. It's just not real."

"Not real," she repeated, feeling oddly numb and very foolish.

"I thought I explained to you exactly where I stand on the whole *falling-in-love* thing. I don't trust it. All *falling* means to me is that a guy is likely to get badly broken when he hits the ground."

"I see," she said carefully, stalling for time— time to figure out some graceful direction to take with this, time to let the awful feeling of outright rejection pass.

He drew in a breath, then released it slowly. "Now you're pissed off at me."

Was she? "Not at all."

His expression turned hopeful, so much so that she ached for him. And how could she judge him for his fear of falling? Until recently—until *him*—she would have said that she felt the same, that falling in love had given her nothing but heartbreak.

"You're not angry, then?" he asked.

Easy and calm, she thought. It was the best way to go right now. "No, I'm not angry. But, of course, I have feelings for you. And I'm not denying them. I care for you, Miles. I care for you deeply."

Talk about a wuss-out. *I care for you deeply?*

No, it wasn't exactly a lie. But it was a million miles from the whole truth. It was the tip of the iceberg, because what she felt for him went so much deeper.

But if he couldn't stand to hear words of love from her mouth, well then, she wouldn't say them.

He watched her way too intently. "I just want to be sure we're still on the same page about this."

The same page?

Oh, they were. They definitely were. He'd just completely refused to love her. She got that message loud and clear. She was right on that page with him, and she hated it.

Did he know he was being a jackass?

Maybe he did, because then he said, "I'm

sorry." He watched her so somberly. "I do think the world of you."

She believed him.

He thought the world of her—he just couldn't love her.

What to say now? She settled on a gentle "I understand."

He pulled her close again and kissed her. She let him, but she didn't really kiss him back.

He asked, "Tired?"

She nodded up at him, then eased away to turn off the lamp.

All the next day, Josie took special care to put on a smile, to behave as if nothing had changed.

But inside, she felt awful. Hurt. Wounded by her own love.

Okay, maybe she *was* in the wrong here. She'd known what she would have with him when she'd said yes to him. As he'd reminded her so painfully last night, they had an agreement. She'd married him with her eyes wide open. At the time, she'd felt the same as he did, that falling in love was just asking for trouble.

She needed to keep her mouth shut, respect the deal they'd made when they started. She and Miles had it all. She didn't need words of love to make her life complete.

The next night, when Miles took her in his

arms and did amazing things to her body, she reminded herself of all that they shared. It was a good life—a great life. She just needed to stop wanting what he'd never agreed to give.

Payton and the twins arrived on the sixth of May, as planned.

The next day, they did the market together, Josie and her little sister in the new, expanded booth that was half Halstead Farm, half Wild Rose. Penn and Bailey played hide-and-seek under the farm tables while Davy slept in his sling against her heart.

They'd had meetings—Zoom calls and one last one in person the night before—to agree on how to handle running two booths as one. It just wasn't efficient to combine the booths and then make shoppers pay the farms separately. They'd decided that they would use one mobile payment account and one cashbox and split the take between the two farms. This season at the market would be an experiment. If the split turned out to be equal to or better than the year before for both farms, they would go on this way.

The market, after all, was something of a side gig for the two farms. It boosted their profiles in the community and brought in extra cash. If combining the two booths worked out, one person could run the whole thing in a pinch.

Business was gratifyingly brisk. Customers remarked how having double the produce in one booth made shopping all the easier.

People they knew stopped by not only to get fresh arugula, spinach, asparagus and free-range eggs, but also to remark on how big the twins had grown, to ask Payton how her current book was going and to coo over Davy. To Josie, they offered their best wishes on her recent marriage to Miles. Josie smiled and thanked them and tried not to feel sad at the reminder that she'd come to want more from Miles than he'd ever been willing to give.

Really, she needed to snap out of this love funk she'd fallen into. It made no sense to be a sad sack. She treasured her life with Miles, and she didn't need his declaration of undying adoration to be happy.

After the market closed, they tallied up. So far, the joint booth was a great success. Both farms would take home more than they had at a first market of the season in the past several years.

With help from Kyle and Tom Huckston, who'd been selling Huckston Honey a few booths down, they loaded up the two trucks and headed for home. Payton led the way and Josie honked goodbye as she took the turnoff to Halstead Farm, where Rafe and Miles were waiting to unload everything.

Miles opened the driver's door for her. "How'd it go?"

"Really well." She told him how much they'd brought in, and he grinned in approval.

About then, Davy started fussing.

"Take him on inside," said Miles. "We'll deal with the truck."

Inside, she put the cash in the office safe. In Davy's room, she'd just settled in the rocker to nurse Davy with Tink at her feet when Payton called.

"Easton arrived an hour ago," her sister said. "Come on over for steaks tonight. The weather's nice. We can eat outside. Bring the girls and invite Rafe."

Ashley begged to go into town for a party with her school friends and to spend the night at Aurora's. Miles let her go, but the rest of them went over to Wild Rose.

It was a great evening and Josie thoroughly enjoyed it...until Payton got her alone in the kitchen before dinner and whispered how good it was to see her and Miles so completely in love. "Miles can't take his eyes off you," Payton added with a knowing smirk.

Josie's heart ached a little harder at her sister's words. Those words gave her hope, and she didn't trust hope right at the moment.

She focused on playing the happy, confident bride. "Me and Miles. Who knew, huh?"

Her sister grabbed her and hugged her. "I felt so bad when I left you here alone and moved to Seattle."

Josie pulled back and gave Payton a stern look. "We talked about that. I told you to go."

"And I did go. And even though I knew you didn't blame me for leaving you—that you really did want me to go, to be happy—I still felt guilty. But not anymore. I mean, think about it."

"O-kay," Josie said on a rising inflection, then confessed, "I have to no idea where you're going with this."

"Well then, I'll tell you. If I'd been here the night Davy was born the way I was supposed to be, you wouldn't have been forced to go to Miles for help."

"Oh, please. Do not blame yourself. That I went to Miles was not your fault. Even without you or Auntie M here, I would've just called an ambulance—if only I hadn't forgotten where I put my phone."

Payton scoffed. "That is so not my point."

"There's a point?"

"Yes, and the point is this. You and Miles have known each other forever and nothing ever happened between you...until you needed help when you went into labor. And had I been here, phone or no phone, you never would have ended up pounding on Miles's door. You two needed to be thrown together in a highly charged situation. And the night that Davy was born, you finally were."

"Come here a minute."

Payton stepped closer. "What?"

Josie grabbed her and gave her a noogie.

"Ouch! Let me go!" Payton pinched her. Laughing, Josie let go and Payton demanded, "Now, tell me I'm right."

"Okay, okay. You're right."

"Of course I am. Miles lives less than a mile from here. But if I'd been at my cottage when you went into labor, you never would've been forced to ask him for help. And you never would've fallen in love with him."

Josie's laughter died in her throat.

Fallen in love. It sounded so good. Until you added the part where he refused to love her back.

What was it about her? What did she lack that would make a man love her? How many times had she given her heart and her trust only to have it tossed right back in her face?

Payton asked softly, "Josie, what is it? Are you all right?"

Josie drew herself up. No way was she breaking down right now. "I *am* all right, yes. More than all right. And you no longer feel guilty for going to Seattle, correct?"

For a moment, Payton had that look she got when she knew something wasn't adding up. But then she nodded. "Correct. I don't feel guilty anymore. I feel good that you've found the love you deserve, that you're with the right man for you."

Too bad I'm not the right woman for him.

Miles had already found that woman, and she had screwed him over but good.

Across the living area, the front door opened. Penn stuck his head in. "Mom! Dad says the steaks are ready!"

Payton gave Josie a wry smile and handed her a big bowl of German potato salad to carry out to the table. "We're on our way!"

Outside, Easton and Payton had put up a canopy tent over the long farm table out on the central lawn between the cottages. They all sat down to eat.

Josie, Miles and Hazel took turns holding Davy. Hazel fed him a bottle, then Josie took him and went inside to change him.

He fell asleep as she was pressing the tabs on a clean diaper. She put him in the soft-sided playpen Payton had brought over from Auntie M's cottage and left the front window open so that she could hear him if he woke.

When she went back outside, everyone was laughing, telling stories, having a great time.

Miles played his part as a doting new husband,

putting his arm across Josie's shoulders, kissing her cheek, pouring her a second glass of wine without her even having to ask for one.

Easton grinned across the table at them. "You two are such *newlyweds*. Always smooching and giving each other long, steamy looks…"

Miles looked at her adoringly, like she was the love of his life. "Hey. It's what newlyweds do." And he grabbed her and kissed her right there at the table for everyone to see.

For a guy who refused to love her, he was pretty good at pretending he did.

Josie played along and kissed him back. Their life together was so damn good.

She should be satisfied.

But she wasn't. She needed to do something, *change* something.

She just hadn't decided yet what that change should be.

Chapter Ten

Easton went home the next day. Payton stayed on that night and Monday night. The original plan had been for her to remain at the farm for a couple of weeks, to help with chores and whatnot, and be there for at least two market days.

But Josie had Miles and two first-rate farm-hands to ensure they stayed on top of things at Wild Rose. She'd already talked to both of her stepdaughters, and they'd agreed to switch off every other weekend helping out at Saturday market. Miles, Rafe or Clark would drive the second truck back and forth when Hazel took her turn. Both girls would see a boost in their allowances for adding market days to the chores they already tackled around the farm. There was just no need for Payton to stay longer. She and the twins left for Seattle on Tuesday morning.

That afternoon, as Josie pulled a load of work clothes from the dryer in the utility room, she heard the garage door go up. A few minutes later, Ash and Hazel came in lugging their backpacks.

"Where's Miss Edith?" Hazel demanded.

"Not in here," replied Josie, setting aside the full dryer basket and turning to move the next load from the washer into the now empty dryer.

"Okay then." Hazel was all business. "I'm going to go find Miss Edith, give her some hugs, then change into work clothes and head over to Wild Rose. I want to check on that mule." The rescue barn and pen had a new guest, an old molly named Lulu. "I'll spend some time with Deke and Dotty, too." The two spotted ponies belonged to Penn and Bailey, gifts from their doting grandpa, Myron Wright. "And I'll ask Clark if he needs a hand with anything."

"Sounds good." Josie shut the dryer door and started the cycle. "Back by five thirty?"

"I'll be here." Hazel left.

Ash, however, dropped her pack by the door and stepped up to help Josie fold the load of warm clothes. Josie sent her a smile of thanks. "Good day at school?"

Her beautiful stepdaughter sent her a look from under her thick, dark eyelashes. "It didn't completely suck."

"So, a great day then."

Ashley scoffed. "Yeah. Pretty much." They folded and stacked in companionable silence for a minute or two, then Ash spoke up in a tone both careful and casual. "So about you and Dad...?"

"What about us?"

With painstaking precision, Ashley folded a paint-stained sweatshirt. "I have questions..."

Josie's heart gave a lurch in her chest—one she staunchly ignored. No way her stepdaughter guessed that Miles couldn't give her the kind of love she longed for. "Questions about what?"

"Well, I mean, how do you know when a guy is 'the one'?"

Josie could hear the air quotes around those last two words—and she also felt relief that this was nothing to do with her and Miles's romantic differences. She slid a glance at Ash. Their gazes met and held.

"No," Ash insisted strongly, heavy on the attitude. "I don't have a boyfriend and there's no one I'm interested in, so please don't say anything to Dad about this, 'kay?"

"Not a word," Josie promised.

Yeah, there probably *was* a special guy. Ash had it all—brains, a big heart, a lot of confidence and her mother's knockout good looks. The boys had to be falling all over themselves trying to get her attention. Miles, like most dads with daughters, made it painfully clear that he wished he could forbid her to date until she was at least thirty. No way that was going to happen.

And Josie saw no reason to go running to Miles over a simple conversation between her and Ashley.

Ash lifted a shoulder in a dismissive half shrug. "I've been, you know, thinking about relationships lately, wondering about guys and what it's like, when you find a guy who's different from the rest of them. I'm just asking for future reference…"

"You're wondering how I knew your dad was the one for me?"

"Yeah. That."

Josie matched and folded a pair of heavy socks as she considered her answer carefully. Oddly enough, it was the first time she'd found a bit of comfort in her newfound romantic love for her husband. At least she didn't have to try to talk about something she didn't feel. "I don't know which drew me to him first—all of your dad's wonderful personal qualities or all the stuff we have in common."

Ash wrinkled up her pretty nose. "So it's because he's a good guy and you're both farmers?"

"Well, yes. But more. So much more. There's

also a certain connection between us, a feeling that we understand each other. Sometimes we don't even need words. And then there's the, er, physical attraction. He's handsome and so capable. He's very serious a lot of the time, but he's funny, too—or he can be when he lightens up."

Another scoff from Ash. "At least he lightens up with you occasionally. What else?"

"We want the same things in life."

"You already said that you have a lot in common."

"Fair enough—he's good, a good man."

"You said that, too."

"More than good. Good to the core. And, did I mention, he's superhot?"

Ash let out a sound that could only be called dismissive. "Ugh. So you find my dad to be like the perfect specimen of a man?"

"Well, yeah. I do. But it's not only all his great qualities."

Ashley outright groaned. "Oh, God. There's more..."

"You bet there is. It's about respect. About admiring a man. About knowing I can trust him. I can count on him. I have zero doubt that if I were about to fall off a mountain, he would catch me before I fell, and no matter what, he wouldn't let go."

Ash was hiding a smile. A sideways glance

showed Josie the telltale twitch at the corner of her mouth.

"Did I answer your question?" Josie asked.

"Well…"

Josie poked her with an elbow. "More information than you needed, huh?"

"Maybe a little."

A minute later, Ash finished folding the last faded T-shirt. "I've got some English homework I should deal with…"

Josie nodded. "Thanks for the help."

Ash grabbed her pack and headed for the stairs. For several minutes, Josie gazed out the window over the utility-room sink. As she stared, she thought about all the sterling qualities her husband possessed—all the wonderful things about Miles that made him the man for her. Listing them for Ash had brought everything into focus, somehow. At last, she knew what she needed to do.

She needed to tell Miles she loved him.

Once the truth was out of her mouth, once he understood how much he meant to her…well, that would be it. The edgy, incomplete feeling she lived with lately would fade.

No, she wouldn't go expecting any particular response from him. He did not have to say it back. Hoping that he might would get her nowhere. She just needed him to know what she felt in her heart.

Stacking the folded clothes in the laundry basket to put away, she reassured herself she wasn't under any pressure. It might take her a while to work up the nerve. Which was fine. Great. No reason she necessarily had to rush it. She would do it when she was ready and not before.

That same night, as they got ready for bed, he gave her one of those special smiles of his, a smile both fond and intimate. Right then, she thought she might do it. But the moment passed.

She woke on Wednesday morning with her love still held close inside her, unshared. Wednesday night in bed, she almost got there. She was lying with her head on Miles's broad chest, listening to the steady cadence of his heart, thinking this was it. The moment had come.

"Miles, I've been meaning to—"

"Dad, Josie!" Hazel, her voice tight with panic, pounded on the bedroom door. "I can't find Miss Edith!"

Miles called, "Did you check behind the dryer?"

"I did! She's not in the utility room. I can't find her anywhere!"

So they got up and helped her look. Ashley joined the search, too. They scoured the house, from top to bottom, including the garage, the screen porch in the back and the office, too.

A half an hour later, the four of them converged in the front hall, where both Tink and Bruce were whining and sniffing at the door.

They all figured it out simultaneously.

"You think she's…?"

"Wait. She couldn't be…?"

Miles ordered the dogs to sit and pulled open the door.

Miss Edith waited on the other side, her eyes low and lazy, her fluffy tail curled around her front paws and her purr loud enough for everyone to hear.

"There you are!" Hazel scooped the kitten up in her arms and scolded her as she carried her toward the great room and the stairs.

Then, from the baby's room at the back of the house, they heard Davy crying. Ash followed Hazel up the stairs and Josie went to get the baby. As for her love, she left it undeclared for another night.

Thursday night, she made certain Davy was sound asleep when she left him in his new room. Lingering a bit, she admired the new farm mural she'd stenciled the week before. This one was even cuter than the one at her cottage on Wild Rose. She'd added a few extra spotted cows, more flowers, bees and butterflies, along with a bigger barn and a family of goats. The room looked great with all the furniture and baby gear in place.

And Davy hadn't stirred as she admired his new room. With any luck, he would sleep for several hours.

Josie went upstairs and looked in on Hazel, who was lying on her bed with Miss Edith cuddled beside her and her tablet on her lap.

"'Night, Haze."

"'Night, Josie."

She found Ashley in her room fiddling on her phone.

"Don't play all night," she said.

Ash blew her a kiss and gave her a thumbs-up. Josie kind of marveled at how well she and Ashley got along. Miles, on the other hand, often found himself in deep water with his older daughter. Sometimes anything he said would set her off. An offhand remark like, "nice weather," could have Ashley jumping all over him.

But Ash never seemed to get prickly with Josie. She took Josie's suggestions and even the occasional critical remark with good humor and usually a smile.

Josie walked downstairs slowly, her hand gliding along the banister, her tummy a bit swoopy at the prospect of sharing her heart's secrets with Miles. Mentally crossing her fingers, she said a silent prayer—that he wouldn't reject her declaration outright, wouldn't start reminding her about their agreement, warning her that what they shared didn't include falling in love.

In their bedroom, he was already propped up against the pillows. He grinned when she came in.

"If it isn't the woman I can't wait to see naked." He lifted the covers in a welcoming way.

She stripped in a flash and climbed in with him, thinking how easy and fun and relaxed he was around her. Before the fateful night he found her crouched on his doorstep about to have Davy, she'd never seen even a hint of this side of him.

When Fiona was still alive, he'd been that thoughtful, neighborly guy, the one you could always turn to for a favor or in a crisis. And once Fiona died, he became stern and withdrawn.

Never in those earlier times could she have guessed he would one day be her top contender for Sexiest Man on the Face of the Earth.

He kissed her. With a moan of sheer delight, she wrapped her arms around him and sank into that kiss. His big, work-roughened hands moved over her knowingly and so tenderly. With just his touch, he stole all her secrets and claimed them for his own.

Life could be so surprising. Here she'd married him because she really did like him. Because she'd known they would make a good team, a solid partnership. At the time she'd said yes to him, she'd believed their union to be mostly practical. They were farmers who lived next door to each other. Their lives would blend seamlessly, each of them enhancing and enriching the working whole.

She hadn't known the half of it. This man was everything.

With him, her life made sense on every level—head, heart and lower down.

Now she burned for him. She yearned for him. She came to this bed every night with butterflies in her belly and gladness in her heart.

Long fingers glided down her hip, catching her in the curve at the back of her knee. She took his signal and lifted her legs, twining them around him. Her body opened to him, taking him in, all the way, so good and deep.

He buried his face in the curve of her throat. "What you do to me, Josephine. It ought to be illegal…"

She shoved her fingers into his hair and held on. Turning her head, she captured those lips of his and they moved together, slow and then faster. He rolled to his back so that she topped him… and then rolled them again to reclaim the dominant position. He muttered encouragements as she reached for the peak. When she got there, gasping, calling his name, he followed her over the edge.

For a moment, they held on so good and tight.

And then, slowly, they fell back to their separate pillows, both of them still breathing hard, reaching out to clasp hands, laughing a little at the glorious rightness of the life they'd made together.

It was her moment. The one she'd been waiting for.

She turned her head as he turned his. Looking directly into his chambray-blue eyes, she said, "I want you to know that I love you, Miles Halstead. I'm *in* love with you."

He did just what she'd guessed he would—he frowned, a frown that creased the skin between those beautiful eyes. The corners of his mouth tightened a fraction. She knew he was trying to decide how to deal with her gently, how to remind her that they had an agreement, to insist that she knew very well the love thing wasn't part of it.

"Stop," she whispered. "It's okay. I don't need or expect you to say it back. I just need you to know how I feel, where I am in this. I need to be able to tell you what's in my heart."

He already had her hand. Now, he wove his fingers with hers, brought them to his lips and brushed his mouth across her knuckles, causing sparks to flash and flare across her skin. "I think the world of you, Josie. I can't tell you how much I admire you, how happy I am to be with you, to be married to you."

Her smile only trembled a little. "I'm glad."

"And I'm honored. To be the one you love."

She held his eyes and kept on smiling as she tried really hard to keep her promise to herself.

To be happy that he knew her true feelings now... and not to yearn for all the love he refused to give.

But, come on, *honored*?

She knew he meant well. She knew he didn't want to hurt her. And she also believed that he did feel honored to be with her, to have her for his wife. She felt the same about him.

But *honored* wasn't the half of it. It just wasn't.

Okay, yeah, you couldn't make the horse drink once you'd led him to the water, but that didn't keep you from thinking the horse was a damn fool, now did it?

Couldn't he just take the leap and say "I love you"? Hadn't he figured out by now that she was not Fiona, not some schemer who married one man while continuing to keep the other on a string? The questions spun in her mind, each with a clear, easy answer he simply refused to give her.

For the rest of that week and into the next, she kept a bright face on things. She reminded herself of all her husband's admirable qualities, the ones she'd listed in detail to Ashley just the week before. She should be happy.

She had everything but his love. Shouldn't what she had be enough?

Yes, it should, she scolded herself.

But she was human and greedy, and her heart ached for more from him. She probably should have seen this coming when she decided to tell him how she really felt. She should have known all along that his mere acceptance of her love could not make everything better.

Nothing was better. How could it be? She'd given him her heart and he refused to give his in return.

On Friday, a week and a day from the night she told him she loved him and found out how *honored* he was about that, the girls had arranged to remain in town after school. Hazel would go to Donna's. Ashley and Aurora would attend a basketball game, after which Ashley would spend the night with her best friend. Donna would drop Hazel at Saturday market so she could help Josie out.

"Let me take you to dinner tonight," Miles said that morning. He made the offer kind of coaxingly, like he wasn't quite sure she would say yes. Had he noticed that all was not right between them, at least not for her?

She really had tried not to take out her frustrations on him. But they were pretty well attuned to each other, so she couldn't pretend to be surprised that she'd failed to hide her current unhappiness all that well.

"I would love a night out," she said with enthusiasm, trying to push past the hurt in her heart.

Miles called a friend of Hazel's to babysit Davy for a couple of hours.

They went to a great steak place in Hood River. Josie maintained a positive attitude through the meal. She reminded herself yet again of what a fine man he was, how her feelings were hers to deal with. It could in no way be construed as his fault that she now wanted to switch up the rules on him when true love forever had never been part of the plan.

They had wine, a really nice cabernet. She thought maybe the wine would relax her, help her put aside this pointless hurt and frustration she couldn't stop feeling.

The wine did relax her. It also dragged her down even further into her growing funk of melancholy disappointment.

She kept up a pretty good front, though, she thought—all through dinner and the ride back to the farm. While Miles left to take the sitter home, she started to get ready for bed.

In their bathroom, she removed her light makeup and brushed her teeth. As she rinsed her mouth, she caught sight of her reflection in the mirror...and something just snapped.

The next thing she knew, she was dragging a suitcase down from the closet and tossing stuff in it, enough for a few nights. Once she had her bag packed, she filled one for Davy. Miraculously, she packed for him in his darkened room as he slept and somehow managed not to wake him.

The garage door went up as she was tossing the suitcases into the back of her Jeep. In the glare of Miles's headlights, she clicked her tongue at Tink, who jumped in and settled right down.

As Miles's pickup rolled to a stop next to her Jeep, she shut the hatch door and hurried back into the house, headed for the nook of hallway outside Davy's room where she'd left his travel bassinet and diaper bag. She'd just grabbed both items when she heard Miles's footsteps coming in from the utility room.

He spotted her there by Davy's door and stopped, taking in the diaper bag and the folded baby bed before he finally met her eyes. "What's going on, Josie?"

She squared her shoulders and met his eyes. "We have to talk."

He blinked a few times. "I don't get it. What are you doing?"

"Shh." She tipped her head toward Davy's shut door. Might as well not get the baby stirred up, at least not until she had to go in there and pull him out of his bed. Setting the bag and the bassinet back down, she gestured toward the living area.

Miles seemed about to say something, but then he just shook his head, turned on his heel and took an easy chair. She sat on the sofa across from him. "Okay, it's like this. I've tried, Miles. I really have."

He put both arms out to the side, palms up. "Tried to...?"

"Be happy with just loving you. I've tried not to need you to love me back. It's a lot of *try* I've been putting out, I promise you. But it's just not working. We're so close to having it all, but you're holding on so tight to what a dead woman did to you. You can't share your heart when it's all filled up with someone else."

"No." He sat forward, his every movement crackling with carefully banked emotion. "That's not true. My heart is not filled up with the woman who screwed me over."

"Well, it must be filled with something, Miles. Because there's no room in there for me. I mean, what she did to you was terrible. I'm not trying to tell you otherwise. But at some point, you need to let it go, to move on."

"I've moved on," he said darkly. "I've let it go."

"Uh-uh. No. I don't believe that. I don't pretend to know what you've been through, how bad it was for you. But I know my own heart. I know that I gave up, too. After that last time, when Taylor Brentwood dumped me and turned right around and married someone else, I put up walls. I was done with the love thing. Over. Finished. Through."

"Josie, I know. I do understand."

"No. Uh-uh. I don't think you do. Everything

has changed for me, the longer I've been with you. I've slowly come to realize that I'm not through with love and that I love *you*—oh, Miles, I wish I could make you see how it was for me to step beyond my own walls, the ones that I put up on purpose to protect my heart. But I did it. And I need you to do it, too."

"But we agreed that we—"

"Don't you hear me? Aren't you listening? What we agreed before isn't enough for me. What we agreed isn't working. And if you won't do it, if you can't give loving me a chance, then you're showing me that I really don't have your trust. You're showing me you believe that if you let down your guard for me, I'll do you like Fiona did."

He had a look. Like she'd just smacked him in the face. "No. Uh-uh. That's not true."

"Yeah, it is. It hurts, Miles. It hurts a lot, to know you think that of me. It hurts and it's not true. I would never do what she did."

"Josie," he pleaded. "I *don't* think you would do what Fiona did. I know that you wouldn't."

"Good. Because I've thought long and hard about us. I've turned it over and over inside my mind until my head is spinning with it. And the conclusion I've come to is that we're together for the wrong reasons."

"No. Uh-uh. That is not—"

"Stop. Listen. There has to be trust. We both have to take a real chance on each other, on love. I'm grateful to you. I am. You've broken the protective shell I made around my heart. I love what we have, Miles, I do. So much."

His expression had hardened. He scoffed, "And yet you seem to be telling me you're throwing it away."

"Because what we have isn't enough for me anymore."

"Josie, come on." He surged to his feet...and then he seemed not to know what to do with himself once he got there. He shoved his hands in his pockets and glared. "You're making no sense. How can you not know all you mean to me? I like you. I want you. I can't picture my life now without you. You *have* me. What more can you want from me?"

This was going nowhere. "How many different ways can I say it? I love you. I'm *in* love with you. And I want you to let yourself openly love me back. I want the words, Miles. I want to hear those three special words from your mouth because those words belong to me."

"You have no right to do this to me—to us." His voice was low, but so hard, as unyielding as that look on his face. "You know I can't do what you want, I can't say that crap. Never again. And you knew it from the start."

Yes, she did know it. She also knew that a lesser man would just say the damn words and move on, whether he denied them in his heart or not. But Miles couldn't tell that lie. The man was honest, she had to give him that.

And they had nothing more to argue about here. "You're right," she said gently. "I understood your position on this. I accepted it when we got married. But I can't accept it now. *Never again* just doesn't work for me. *Never again* is not an answer when we are talking about love." She stood. They faced off across the coffee table. "I love you, Miles. And right now, I need some space."

He caught her arm as she tried to get past him. Pulling her close to him, he dipped his head to nuzzle her cheek as he whispered desperately, "Please. Don't go."

She looked up at him and she could see it, right there in his eyes, all the love he wouldn't let himself admit to. She wanted to turn toward him, reach for him, melt into those big, strong arms of his.

But where would that leave them?

Right where they were now. "I need some time to myself. I'm going back to Wild Rose for now. Please let go of me."

"Josie…"

"Listen to me. Everything can go on as it has been. We can run the farms together. I'll be here bright and early tomorrow to help load up for the market. I'll be…around, okay? A lot. And I will talk to the girls, explain to them in a simple, non-blaming way that we're having issues, that for the time being I'll be staying over at Wild Rose"

"That's going to really upset them."

"And I'm sorry about that. But I just can't sleep in our bed with you now. I need my own place to go to. I need to be away from you. You need to let me go."

At last, he released her. She went straight for the diaper bag and the folded bassinet waiting in the hallway. Once she had those loaded in the Jeep, she went back for Davy.

By then, Miles had left the great room. She assumed he'd gone to their bedroom at the front of the house, and she felt a sort of sad relief that he wouldn't try again to stop her from leaving.

Davy barely stirred as she gathered him into her arms, but he started crying when she settled him into his car seat. From her spot in the rear, Tink gave an anxious whine.

"It's okay, Tink," she soothed the dog.

But it wasn't okay. Not in the least. And Davy was full-out wailing when she pulled to a stop in front of her deserted cottage at Wild Rose Farm.

Chapter Eleven

She was gone.

Davy, too. Just like that. Miles hardly knew what to do with himself. The house seemed to echo with emptiness.

Bruce trailed around after him as he went through the motions—locking up, turning off lights, brushing his teeth and finally climbing into bed. It was too big, the bed, without her. He grabbed her pillow and buried his face in it, sucking in the echo of her scent, trying to find comfort there.

Finally, he threw the damn pillow across the room. It hit a lamp and the lamp toppled. Maybe it broke. He couldn't quite make himself give a damn. Bruce let out a whimper of worry and confusion.

"I hear you, boy," he said. "Me, too."

A few minutes later, he heard a yowl from the other side of the bedroom door. Apparently, Hazel's kitten didn't want to spend her night alone.

He got up, pulled the door open and picked up the cat. "Sorry. Hazel's visiting her grandma. It's just us tonight." The kitten only looked at him through glowing green eyes. He set it down on the rug and went back to his empty bed, stopping to right the lamp—miraculously unbroken—and snatch up Josie's pillow on the way.

Settling in with his head on her pillow, he shut his eyes and willed himself to sleep. The cat jumped onto the mattress. She didn't come near him and she didn't start purring, just curled up at the foot of the bed. He had a feeling Miss Edith wasn't any happier tonight than he was.

The next morning, Josie arrived as promised, bringing Davy with her, to load up for the market. He had no idea what to say to her, so he kept his mouth shut.

Before she left, he suggested, "There are some bottles of milk left in the fridge. Why not leave him with me while you're gone?"

He waited, his gut twisting, for her to say it wasn't a good idea.

But then she nodded. "Sure."

She gave him the diaper bag and Davy in his car seat, and headed for town, Clark following behind in the other truck. Miles took Davy inside. He put down a play mat and a mobile of airplanes over it and stretched out on the floor beside the cooing baby, feeling marginally better about everything as he watched Davy kick his little feet and make funny baby faces. Later, he took Davy and a bouncy seat out to the shop with him. Davy fell asleep in the seat as Miles worked on a few projects.

When Josie returned in the afternoon, she had Hazel with her. One look in his younger daughter's eyes and he knew that Josie had already talked to her.

Hazel came right to him and hugged him. "I love you, Dad." She sniffled, trying hard not to cry.

He pulled her closer. "And I love you," he whispered against her silky hair.

As Clark got out of the other truck and set to work helping Rafe unload the Halstead Farm tables and crates, Ashley drove up. Josie waved at her and then came straight for him and Hazel.

"Got a minute?" Josie asked.

Hazel trotted over to get her suitcase from the truck, leaving him alone with the woman who had suddenly decided to leave him.

Josie said, "I already told Hazel that I'm staying at Wild Rose for a while."

"Yeah. I figured."

"I don't know how you want to handle this." She kept her voice low. Those big eyes confused him. They seemed full of sympathy and tender understanding. Those eyes made him want to grab on to her and not let go...and simultaneously, to spin on his heel and walk away, to leave her standing there staring after him. "I can stay a bit," she offered. "We can talk to the girls together."

That sounded like pure hell to him. "No. You go ahead. Just leave."

"Are you sure?"

"Positive."

"Okay, then. First though, I'm going to tell Ash that I'm staying at Wild Rose for now and I'll be there any time she wants to talk."

He longed to inform her that she would do no such thing. But he didn't. He gave her a curt nod and nothing more.

Whatever she said to Ashley, it was quick. Ash nodded and they shared a hug.

A few minutes later, Josie and Davy drove off with Clark, at which point Ashley marched right up to him. "Okay, Dad. We need to talk."

The talk happened ten minutes later in the great room. Ashley and Hazel sat on the sofa and Miles took one of the chairs across from them. Hazel had her kitten in her lap. At least Miss Edith was happy. The little cat purred like a motorboat as his daughters sat silent, waiting for him to tell them why their stepmother had moved out.

Miles said the only thing he could think of to say. "Josie's staying at her farm for a while. She needs a little time on her own..." His mind kind of went blank then. He hated this so much and he had no idea what to say next. He really should have taken Josie up on her offer to do this together... but then again, no. It was better this way, just him and the girls.

Ashley demanded, "Why?"

"I just told you, Ash. She needs—"

"Dad. What's going on? This makes no sense, and you know it."

Hazel spoke up then. "She told me just what Dad said. That she needed time. To be by herself, to, um, figure things out. But then she said to come over to see her anytime, and that we could talk about it. She said that she would be over here to see us, too. That we were still a family, she's just staying at Wild Rose for a while."

Ash didn't so much as glance at her sister. "Whatever you did, fix it," she said, glaring at him.

He was not and never had been a hotheaded guy. But right now, it would be so easy to start yelling at Ash. "Look. I didn't want her to go. She said that she needed to go. What could I do?"

"But what *happened*? What made her *need* to go?"

As though he could explain that. As though he could just say "I won't tell her I love her." If he did that, Ash would only ask "Why not?"

And then what?

Uh-uh. No good could come from going down that road.

"Ashley, what happened between Josie and me is not about you. Yes, she and I are having some, er, problems. But we both love you and we are both here for you, for whatever you need."

Eyes narrowing, Ash caught her upper lip between her teeth. "Well, Dad. Then what I need is for you to fix things with Josie so that she will come home. Will you do that?"

"Ashley, I—"

"Got it. Fine. I'm going to my room." She jumped up and flounced off.

Miles rubbed the bridge of his nose in an effort to ease the headache that had started pounding behind his eyes.

Hazel kissed her kitten and set it on the floor. The cat strutted away, purring, its fluffy tail held high. "Come on, Dad. Let's go figure out what to do about dinner..."

An hour later, Ash came out of her room to

set the table, eat and load up the dishwasher. "I'm going to see Josie," she announced once the cleanup was done.

When she returned, he couldn't stop himself from asking her what she and Josie had talked about.

"Nothing new. Just what you said. That she needed time, that she's there for me and Hazel whenever we need her. Is it all right if I go into town?"

He probably should have seen that coming. "Better stay home tonight," he said gently.

She pinched up her mouth at him, but at least she didn't argue.

They got through that evening. And he got through another night in his empty bed.

And another night after that.

Josie came over several times that week. She hung out with the girls. She made sure Miles got to spend time with Davy. She spoke to him about everyday things—the accounts, the big broccoli crop, the weddings she had booked at the Wild Rose event barn.

He waited. For her to come to her senses and come home to him—to them.

But she didn't.

On Saturday, a week and a night after Josie left him, it was Ashley's turn to work the market. She drove the Halstead truck, falling in behind Josie in the Wild Rose truck.

At ten, Miles's mother came by to pick up Hazel for an overnight with her in town. His mom didn't seem to have a clue that his wife had moved out, and Miles didn't tell her. Yeah, he knew that Hazel would say something to her, but he just couldn't bring himself to worry about that until it happened.

When Ashley and Josie got back that afternoon, Ash packed an overnight bag and went to join her grandmother and sister in town. Miles considered asking Rafe and Clark if they wanted to go out for a beer. But he decided against it. He wasn't very good company lately. Plus, once he'd had a few beers, he might say things he shouldn't.

Sunday morning at eleven, he came in from the cherry orchard to grab a quick sandwich and spotted his mother's SUV parked out in front. He found her at the kitchen counter plating paninis.

"I did knock," she explained. "When you didn't answer, I figured you were out working, so I used my key."

The muscles at the back of his neck drew tight. "No problem." Not about her letting herself in the house, anyway.

"Lunch?" she offered with a cheery smile as she carried the plates to the table. "Iced tea? Lemonade?"

His stomach rumbling at the sight of the sandwich, he went to the sink to wash up. "The tea is great. You're here alone?"

She was already at the fridge. As she pulled the door wide and grabbed the pitcher of tea, she said, "The girls went to Aurora's for a bit. I thought you and I might have a little talk." She had that look, eyes flinty, mouth set. He knew his own mother. She would not leave the farm until she'd had her say.

Miles dried his hands and took his place at the table. A moment later, his mother set tall glasses of iced tea beside each of their plates. "Eat. Don't let that panini get cold."

He ate a couple of bites of the excellent sandwich and sipped a little tea.

It didn't take Donna long to get down to business. "I talked to the girls. They said Josie's staying at Wild Rose now."

"Yes, she is, Mom. And I really don't want to talk about this."

"All right. I'll do the talking and you can just sit there and listen and think about the things I have to say."

Where did she get the idea that trying to eat lunch while she lectured him was a plan he could get behind? "It's not your business. You know it's not."

"*You* are my business. And so are the girls.

When you're not happy, I'm not happy. And I will never forgive myself if I don't speak up when I see you throwing away your happiness with both hands."

He resisted the need to inform her that *he* had not done the throwing, that Josie was the one who'd walked out. His mom would only do what Ashley did—ask him what *he'd* done to make Josie leave.

That question he would never answer. It was between Josie and him. His mother and his older daughter needed to butt the hell out of his relationship with his wife.

"I just don't understand you, Miles. You've finally got a wonderful wife who loves you openly and honestly, and yet somehow, you're determined to screw it all up."

He shouldn't ask. He *wouldn't* ask.

But then he did ask. "What do you mean, I've *finally* got a wonderful wife? What about Fiona? You loved Fiona. You said so more than once."

His mother looked at him so patiently, it made his molars ache. She fiddled with a bit of crust. "Now, Miles. I really hate to speak badly of Fiona..."

He demanded, "What the hell are you talking about, Mom?"

"Settle down..."

"Then explain yourself."

"Well, honey. She was your wife, and I did care for her. But looking back, I always had this weird feeling that there was something…not all there about Fiona. She was gone so much, wasn't she? And I always felt she had her own… Oh, what is the word? Inner life, I suppose you could say, some part of herself she never shared with any of us. I wanted to feel close to her, to be affectionate with her, but I never felt she welcomed my affection."

A shiver, like a trickle of ice water, had started working its way down his spine. *Something not all there about Fiona? A part of herself that she never shared?*

All these years his mother had sensed that something was off with Fiona and yet she'd never bothered to mention it to him? All this time, he'd lived under the mistaken assumption that his mother had adored his first wife.

"You never said a word about any of this before," he accused.

"Of course, I didn't. While Fiona was alive, it seemed wildly inappropriate to criticize your wife and the mother of your children. And then, when she died, well, what possible good could it do to speak ill of the dead?"

"And yet, here you are, speaking ill of her now."

"Don't take that tone with me. There's a *reason* to say these things to you now. Because now you have Josie, who is no Fiona. Josie is open and loving, a breath of fresh air. I walked in this house an hour ago and, well, it just felt empty without her. I miss her presence in this house. The girls miss her."

And I miss her, too! he wanted to shout, while maybe pounding his fist on the table for emphasis.

But he didn't. Instead, he tried to reason his way out of the conversational noose his own mother was tightening around his neck. "Mom. Josie's here almost every day. And when she's not, the girls visit her at Wild Rose."

"What about that little baby? You love Davy."

"Yes, and I see him often. Josie makes sure I get time with him."

"Well, and isn't that just more proof of what a wonderful woman she is?"

"Mom. Yes. Josie is a wonderful woman. And if you want to see her, just go on over to Wild Rose and knock on her door."

"Please, Miles. It's not only that I miss having her here. You have made a family with her. The two of you are just getting started and I honestly believe that you and Josie can have so much together, years and years of happiness. I hate to see you throwing that away. So what if she comes here and the girls go to her at her farm? That's not enough. Josie's the mother those girls always needed, and they need their mom right here at home. And, as the only father he's ever known, little David needs *you*. And speaking of you—"

"Mom. You need to stop."

Donna did no such thing. "You *miss* her." She actually shook a finger at him. "You know you do. Whether you're willing to admit it or not, you need that woman. She is the one for you." His mother leaned toward him, eyes sharp as daggers, like an eagle homing in on its helpless prey. "You're lovesick without her and you need to admit that. It's written all over you, clear as a brand-new day to the rest of us. Whatever's standing in your way, Miles Stanley, you need to get over it and go make things right with your wife."

Josie had just put Davy down for a nap when her phone chimed with a text.

It was Alex.

What's the Halstead family up to this Sunday?

Josie winced as she read the words. She'd yet to tell her sisters or her aunt that she'd packed up and taken her baby back to her cottage on Wild Rose. When she dropped that bomb, they would all come running.

And she just didn't want them to go putting their own lives on hold to support her in yet another time of trial. They'd already come running when Davy was born. They'd helped her throw together a beautiful last-minute wedding and then dropped everything to be there for it. They deserved a longer break before they had to rush to her side to console her now her marriage was in trouble.

And not only did she not want to go crying to her family again, but she was also holding on to the fading hope that she and Miles would work things out before she finally had to admit to the fact that her eight-week-old happily-ever-after had already hit a major snag.

As she stewed over how to answer Alex, the text bubble started moving.

Her sister wrote:

It's Sunday, did you notice? And I don't have to work until tomorrow. I want to see you, hug you, hold my nephew, hang out for a few hours with my step-nieces and my new brother-in-law. Tell me I'm invited for dinner.

So much for her fading hope.

Yes! Come to dinner. I'm at Wild Rose, so come straight to my cottage?

Josie closed her eyes and willed her sister to simply confirm and jump in the car. It would take

Alex about an hour to get here, which meant Josie would have a short reprieve during which she could wrack her brain trying to decide how to explain why she'd left Miles.

But Alex had always been too sharp by half. Josie's phone rang in her hand. She answered with a lackluster "Hi, there."

"What's going on, Josephine?"

"I, um, well, Miles and I are having some problems…"

"What? But I *like* Miles. He's a good guy!"

Josie admitted, "It's not Miles's fault exactly— I mean, it's me as much as him…"

"*What's* not his fault? And never mind. I need to be there. Just sit tight. I'll see you in an hour."

"Wait. Don't hang up yet!"

"What? Speak."

"Do not call Payton or Auntie M. I haven't told them and I'm not having them riding to my rescue, too."

"But Josie, they will want to—"

"Alex. Do. Not. Call. Them."

Alex made a low, frustrated sound. "Duly noted. I'm there in an hour…"

Fifty-six minutes later, her big sister's SUV pulled to a stop just down the walk from where Josie sat on the top step, Tink at her side.

Alex jumped out of the car and Josie ran to meet her. They collided midway up the walk and hugged it out. After Alex greeted Tink, they went inside, at which point Davy woke from his nap and quickly progressed from fussing to crying.

Josie sat at the table to nurse him while Alex made herself coffee.

"Tell me everything," Alex demanded when she took the chair across from Josie.

Josie did exactly that—except for the details concerning Fiona. That was a story only Miles should ever tell. Josie simply said that Miles had been honest with her from the first. Miles had explained to her early on that he'd been hurt badly in love and that he refused to go there again. "At the time, I said I felt the same, that I didn't believe in love anymore, either. We agreed that we didn't need all the love crap to be happy. Instead, we would be best friends and partners in life."

"Wait a minute." Alex poured herself more coffee. "So you're trying to tell me that you married him for every reason but love?"

"I *am* telling you that."

"And I don't believe you. I was there, at your wedding. The two of you have it all going on. Fireworks. Commitment. So much in common. You were in love with him the day you married him, and he felt the same about you."

Josie opened her mouth to argue...and shut it. "I think that maybe you just might be right," she conceded after a moment.

"Of course, I'm right." Alex had never suffered from a lack of confidence in her own opinions. "So the problem is that *you've* faced the truth about how you really feel but Miles hasn't. You've said you love him, but he won't say it back."

Josie groaned. "Why does it sound so silly when you lay it right out like that?"

"It's not silly. Of course, you want your husband, the man you love and have joined your life with, to love you back. But you went into this with *both* of you denying your true feelings, am I right?"

"Well, yeah," Josie muttered, feeling more than a little bit foolish at this point. "And now, I've stopped denying how I feel and he hasn't. I'm afraid it's always going to be like this and, Alex, I just want more. I admit it. I'm selfish. I want it all with him."

"And you deserve it all. But..."

Davy chose that moment to let out a loud burp as he popped off Josie's breast. Josie straightened her bra and her shirt and lifted him to her shoulder. Immediately, he started squirming. She slipped a finger under his diaper. He didn't need changing. "Sorry," she said to Alex.

"I'll wait," said her sister. "Do what you need to do."

Rising, Josie carried Davy to the play mat a few feet away. When she laid him down, he seemed content there—for the moment, anyway. She re-joined Alex at the table.

"May I go on?" Alex inquired in a tone that allowed no objections. At Josie's nod, she asked, "Do you think, just possibly, that you're pushing Miles too fast, that it's hard for you to be patient with him because you've been disappointed in love yourself and you're terrified it might be hap-pening again?"

"Well, and guess what? It *is* happening again."

"Josie, *you're* the one who left, and when I had you on the phone earlier, you took special care to tell me that this situation isn't all Miles's fault."

"Great," Josie groaned. "Use my own words against me."

"Did you say those words or not?"

"Fine. Yes. I said them. Miles isn't the only one with issues around love."

"And all I'm trying to get you to consider is what everybody else already knows. Your hus-band does love you, even if he's having trouble saying it. I just don't want you to throw away a really good thing, that's all. He's a man worth having, a quality guy. He just needs time to get over whatever's holding him back, then he can say what you need to hear."

Miles had watched his mother drive off at twelve thirty. Trying really hard not to think about all the disturbing things she'd said, he had rejoined Rafe and they got back to work.

As the afternoon wore on. Miles focused on each task at hand and refused to wonder how it could be that his mom had always known there was something off with Fiona and yet *he'd* never guessed until her lover told him as they stood at her grave.

At around four thirty, he returned to the house. Leaving his dirty boots on the back step, Miles went in through the screen porch and washed up in the utility room.

When he entered the great room, he found Ashley standing in the living area.

"Hey, Ash. Welcome home. Where's Hazel?"

She gave him a cool shrug. "Upstairs putting her stuff away, playing with Miss Edith. Whatever. I don't know." He fully expected her to launch into her usual thousand reasons why she just *had* to go back into town. Instead, she said, "Can we talk a minute, Dad?"

"Of course." He gestured toward the sitting area. She marched over and sat in one of the chairs. He took the couch. "What's up?"

She flopped back in the easy chair and then leaned forward, like whatever she had on her mind really bothered her, made her antsy, unable to sit still. "Grandma was here, right?"

"Yes, she was." Dread twisted in his stomach

as he realized Ash knew what his mom had come to talk to him about.

"She talked to you about Josie."

It wasn't a question, and he knew that whatever he said next wouldn't be right. It hurt, damn it, just thinking about Josie. It hurt not having her here. It hurt wondering if she would ever come back home to them—to *him*.

"Dad? Did Grandma talk to you about Josie, or not?"

"Yes. Yes, she did."

"Well, so, when are you going to make up with her, Dad? When are you going to make it right with her? She loves you, Dad. Do you even know that?"

"Ash, I…"

"It's a simple question, Dad. Do you know that Josie loves you?"

"Of course."

"Then you need to go get her. I miss her. So does Hazel. You miss her, too—don't you? I think you love her just like she loves you. Or are you going to try to tell me I'm wrong, that you don't actually love your own wife?"

His daughter was so far from wrong. He wanted Josie back, too. But Josie wanted what he couldn't give her, all the words you're supposed to say. The words he *had* said, all the time, back when. The words that were said back to him—every one of them a bald-faced lie. "Ash. Come on. You know you can go over to Wild Rose and see her any-time you want to."

"No, Dad." Ashley's big eyes gleamed with un-shed tears. "That's not good enough. I'm sixteen years old. I need what I never had until Josie. Someone who's here. Someone who cares. Some-one who listens. Someone who understands. I know you try, Dad. And you're a good dad, you are. But there's really no substitute for a good mom."

What was she telling him? "I'm sorry, honey. So sorry you lost your mom. I know you loved her so much and when she died, you missed her. I un-derstand that you didn't know how to deal with—"

"Wait. No. This is not about my real mother. I mean, come on, Dad. You know how she was. She was gone so much of the time, off selling drugs to pharmacies or whatever. Yes, I loved her. I wor-shipped her. But I never could really get her atten-tion. She never understood me. She was too busy.

"She never *listened* to me the way Josie does. Yeah, I followed her around like a—a little lost puppy, hoping the time would finally come when she would notice me. And, yeah, when she died, I felt like it was a big joke on me, just trailing around after her, hoping and waiting and waiting some more for something that never happened. Instead, she died, and I felt like crap for being so mad at her because she never did hear me. She never did just…stand in the utility room and fold clothes with me and answer my questions. She never did just talk to me and *listen* to what I had to say."

Miles had that feeling a man gets now and then, a feeling that he should pay better attention, that he had it all wrong. That he thought he knew stuff no one else knew, that there were big secrets he had to keep because the people he loved couldn't deal with the truth if somehow the truth got away from him and they found out about it.

He'd thought he'd kept the secret of who Fiona never really was, that he'd protected the people he loved from the ugly truth. But the truth had somehow leaked out, anyway—enough of it that his mother had noticed something "not right" with Fiona. Enough that Ash had felt neglected and ignored by the woman who had given her life.

It struck him right then like a punch to the gut that the day might very well come when his daughters would want—even need—to know the truth about their mom.

But what was that truth? He just couldn't see how finding out about Andrew Walker would help his daughters in any way. What did a kid ever need to know about her dead mother's longtime affair? Maybe if it had turned out that Walker actually was their biological father…

It hadn't, though. And Miles couldn't see how telling them that their mother had cheated, broken her marriage vows, would do anyone any good.

Trying to figure it all out made his head swim, and a longing for Josie swept over him, to have her beside him right now. To know that later, when they were alone, just the two of them, they could talk it over, decide together what needed to be said to the girls, and when to say it.

"Dad! Are you even *listening* to what I'm trying to tell you?"

He blinked and his angry daughter came into focus. She glared at him, furious now. Could he mess up this moment any more completely than he already had? "Yes. Yes, of course I'm listening. I'm sorry, Ash. I just…"

She shot to her feet. "You're just sitting there is what you're doing, sitting there staring at nothing, not hearing a word that I'm saying…"

Just like her mother used to do to her. He got up, too—got up with his hands out, desperate to soothe her, to fix all the hurt parts of her he seemed to keep breaking. "Please, honey. That's not what I—"

"Look." Her face had gone blank, her eyes flat. "Forget it. Just…never mind."

"Ash, come on…"

"I'm going to my room."

"Look, I'm sorry, I—"

"Dad." She waved at him, a dismissive, tired gesture. "Please just let me go."

He did let her go. He'd blown it and he knew it. Better to leave her alone for a bit and try again later.

She ran up the stairs. He waited for the sound of her bedroom door slamming. Instead, faintly, he heard the door click shut. That was so much worse, somehow, that quiet little click. It said that she didn't even have the heart to slam her door good and hard on him, that all her usual fire and fury had turned into disappointment and defeat.

"Dad?" Hazel asked in a small voice.

He turned from gazing blankly out the kitchen window, a knife in one hand, a raw chicken thigh in the other. His daughter stood on the far side of the island that marked off the living area, her kitten cradled against her chest.

"Hey," he said. "Just getting going on dinner."

Hazel petted Miss Edith, who as usual purred good and loud for such a little thing. "Dad, I heard most of what you and Ash said a little while ago. I stood at the top of the stairs while you were talking. I know that listening to other people's private conversations is bad, but Ash and I agreed that she would talk to you about Josie coming home. Because we both really want Josie back with us, where she belongs. Even Grandma wants that. We miss Josie a lot. And we miss Davy, too."

This kid. Such a loving, tender heart. And so much integrity. She astonished him sometimes. "I know you miss Josie. And in this case, I understand why you listened in."

"Thanks," she said in a small voice, nuzzling the kitten.

In the face of such truthfulness, well, maybe he needed to put a little honesty out there, as well. "I miss Josie, too...and Davy." He hadn't held that little boy in a couple of days now, not since Friday, when Josie had come over to hang out with the girls. After she left, he'd gone and stood in the back bedroom and stared at that farm mural she'd made and hated how empty it felt in there.

Hazel wrinkled her nose at him. "You should go get her. You should say sorry for...whatever happened, and then tell her how much you love her."

Somehow, his thirteen-year-old daughter knew more about relationships than he did.

Hazel dipped to a crouch and set down the kitten. Miss Edith sashayed over to Bruce's water bowl for a drink. "You don't have to say anything, Dad. Just, you know, think about it."

"I will. I mean that." He thought about it all the time now, more so every day. "Did you talk to your sister after she went upstairs?"

"Well, she went past me without a word when

she came upstairs, so I tapped on her door. She said, 'Please go away, Haze.'"

He needed to face it. He sucked as a dad. "Sorry, honey. Maybe we should give her a little time to herself?"

"Good idea."

He dared a step toward her. With Haze, one step was all it took. She darted straight at him, wrapped her arms around his waist and hugged him hard. "I love you, Dad."

"And I love you." He returned her hug as best he could with a chicken part in one hand and a knife in the other. When she let him go, he brandished the chicken thigh. "Help me get dinner on?"

"Sure." She stepped around him, headed for the sink to wash her hands.

When the food was ready, he went up and knocked on Ash's door. A minute later, she opened the door a crack and granted him a scowl. "I just need to be alone."

"Dinner's ready. Come on down and—"

"I'm not hungry."

He truly did not want another fight with her. "I'll have your sister bring you up a plate."

"No, thanks." She shut the door in his face.

He raised his hand to knock again—loudly—but then let it drop to his side. If she needed time, fine. Skipping a meal wouldn't hurt her.

When he got back to the great room, Hazel gave him a look full of sympathy. "Not coming down, huh?"

He shook his head.

They shared a mostly silent meal.

And that night, same as all the nights since Josie left him, he lay awake. He worried about Ash. And he longed for Josie. He wanted his life back—wanted his *wife* back.

But that wouldn't happen until he could say "I love you" honestly. With feeling.

There really was something wrong with him, he decided. Something deeply twisted and not very bright. He wanted Josie and Davy back. Now. And yet, still he held out against giving her those three little words that would bring her home to him.

Because of Fiona. Because of his pride. Because his first wife had lied and she'd cheated, and he'd never had a damn clue until Andrew Walker confronted him at her grave. While Fiona was his wife, he'd said the words every chance he got. And Fiona had said them right back to him while all the time carrying on with another man behind his back.

The signs *had* been there. And he'd spent his whole marriage to her denying those signs. He'd wanted his marriage to be what his parents had had—good and true, unbreakable. He'd wanted that so desperately that he'd made up a relation-ship he never truly had.

With Josie, it was different. She was loyal, and honest to the core. She would never lead a double life. With her, he'd found the marriage he'd spent all those years with Fiona pretending he had.

And yet, he was knocking himself out stomp-ing all over the life that he loved and wanted. No wonder Ash refused to come out of her room.

He needed to man up, and fast. In the morn-ing, he promised himself, he would fix what he'd broken.

At some point long after midnight, he finally fell into a fitful sleep, only to wake sometime later to the sound of Bruce whining at the bed-room door. He got up, let out the dog and waited on the step for him to do his business, which took a bit. Bruce seemed agitated. He sniffed around, whining. No doubt some critter—a possum or a jackrabbit—had gotten up on the porch earlier.

Finally, Miles ordered the dog inside and in-structed, "Bed."

Bruce gave it up and went to his bed.

Miles eventually fell asleep again...and woke with a start at 5:00 a.m. He was halfway out of bed, ready to put on some work clothes and get going on morning chores, when he realized it was Rafe's day for that.

With a groan, he flopped back to his pillow,

put a hand across his eyes and waited for sleep to find him again.

Didn't happen. At a little after six, he gave up. Climbing from the tangled bed, he pulled on jeans and a T-shirt. With Bruce at his heels, he wandered out to the main room to get the coffee going…and found Ashley's note waiting on the counter next to the coffee maker.

Chapter Twelve

Dad,

I've had it. I can't deal with you anymore. I want my own life with the man I love. Chase and I are leaving, making a new start together free of all the garbage and hassle of adults with their rules and judgments.

I mean seriously, how can we even do things like you say when it's superclear that you're just stumbling through life like everyone else, making a mess of things, wrecking your own happiness AND the happiness of your daughters?

It's enough. I am so done. Chase is picking me up and taking me away from here. I love you and I love Haze, but I am through trying to deal with all that you put me through.

Ash

Miles shut his eyes and drew in three slow, careful breaths. Then he spun around and raced up the stairs to the open door of Ashley's room. She wasn't in there. He stared at her neatly made bed, at her wide-open closet door, where empty hangers dangled from the rod.

With Bruce close behind him, he crossed the hall and silently peeked in on Hazel—still there and sound asleep. Did she know anything about this?

Carefully, he shut her door. Before he woke her, he needed to try to reach Ashley.

He ran down the stairs to his room, snatched his phone off the night table and autodialed Ash. It went straight to voice mail. He waited for the tone. "Ash. Just call me. Just call me when you get this. Please."

And then he hung up and called Josie.

She answered on the first ring. "What's going on?" She sounded wide-awake, but then, she was a farmer, and it was after six in the morning. "Is everyone all right?" Just the sound of her beautiful voice—kind. Competent. Calm. It helped. "Miles. Come on. Talk to me…"

"It's Ash. She ran off last night. She left a note…"

"I'll be right over."

"Josie, she's got a boyfriend. Some guy named Chase. Did you know?"

"No, I didn't. And listen, I'm on my way. I'll be there. Ten minutes."

"Yeah. Now. Please."

When she arrived in her Jeep, he ran out to meet her, Bruce following close at his heels.

Josie parked in the driveway, got out, pulled open the back door and unhooked Davy in his car seat. Tink jumped out, too. Bruce went straight for her. There was sniffing and whines of greeting.

Miles started toward his wife and barely managed to pull himself up short a couple of feet from her. She looked so good, her cheeks flushed beneath those cute freckles, her hair in a gorgeous tangle, piled up on her head, little corkscrews escaping every which way. Even the tired shadows under her eyes were beautiful to him.

"Hi," she said.

"Hi. Thanks for coming."

"Any news?" she asked breathlessly.

He shook his head.

"We'll find her," she promised.

He stepped forward, wanting to grab her close,

but stopped himself just in time. "Let me take Davy. You get the diaper bag."

She handed over the car seat.

"Good to see you, little man," he said to the baby, who stared up at him, wide-eyed, making little grunting sounds as he tried to stick his whole fist in his mouth.

Miles led the way inside, where the dogs flopped down on the floor next to each other and Davy kept gumming his hand.

"The note?" Josie asked.

"Right there, on the counter."

She grabbed it and read it through quickly. "So…she's angry at you?"

"Yeah. We had an argument last night. She misses you."

"And she blames you for that?"

"Yeah. Yeah, she does. And she's not wrong." He had so much more to say, so much to make right. If only it wasn't too late. If only Josie would give him a chance to fix what he'd broken.

But all the things he had to say would have to wait. Right now, they had a more urgent priority. "I don't know what to do, Josie. Is she safe? Dear God, is she pregnant? Doing drugs? Where are they going? How will they live?"

"Did you try her cell?"

"Yeah. She didn't answer. I left a voice mail."

Josie pulled out her phone and typed out a

quick text. "I'm just asking her to check in with me..."

For a moment after she hit Send, they just stood there staring down at her phone.

She met his eyes with a sigh. "No reply—you have any idea when she left?"

"Not for sure, but Bruce woke me up whining to get out at a little after two. I'm thinking he heard her leave." Anxious energy pulsed through him. After carefully setting the car seat on the island, he started walking. Five long strides later, he turned around and came back. "What next? Where is she? We need to find her. We need to..."

Her fingers closed around his arm. "Breathe."

He froze in midstep. "I'm trying." He looked down at her hand—holding him, steadying him—and then back up into her eyes. "What next?"

"Is Hazel here?"

"Yeah. In bed..." Panic tried to cut off his air again. "Or she was, a little while ago..."

Josie let go of his arm and took Davy from the car seat. "Grab the note, please. Let's go find out if she knows anything about where Ashley went."

When they reached the top of the stairs, she whispered, "Quietly, okay? Try not to scare her."

"Right." He tapped on the door and carefully modulated his voice as he called, "Hazel?" Slowly, he pushed it open.

"Huh? Yeah?" Hazel sat up. "What?" Yawning, she covered her mouth with her hand and blinked at them as her kitten jumped down from the bed and strutted around them and out the door into the upstairs hall. Hazel rubbed her eyes. "Josie? Davy?" She swung confused eyes his way. "What's going on, Dad? You look totally freaked." She shifted her focus to Josie again…and then she smiled. "Wait. I get it. You guys are back together." She slapped her hand over her heart and cried, "I'm so glad!"

Before Josie could say anything, he wrapped an arm across her shoulders and answered fervently, "Me, too, honey. I'm so glad Josie's here." Josie gaped up at him. He said, looking right in her wide golden-brown eyes, "I've missed you so much." She gave him a trembling smile. He made himself turn to his daughter and focus on the issue at hand. "And right now, Haze, we really need to know who the hell Chase is."

Hazel's mouth dropped open. "Oh, no. Did something…bad happen?"

"As a matter of fact—"

"Miles." Josie cut him off before he could get rolling. "Please let Hazel read the note."

"Right." He passed Hazel the note and somehow managed to keep his mouth shut while she read it. "Well?"

"Um, Chase Briarton is a junior at Heartwood High. He and Ash hang out with the same group of kids. As for the two of them running away together, well, I knew Ash really liked him, but that they're together, close enough that she would ask him to do something like this? Uh-uh, Ashley didn't tell me about that."

"Briarton." He whipped out his phone. "You have his number?"

"No, Dad. I hardly know him, except that everyone says he's a good guy. He's an A student, *and* an athlete. All the girls are after him."

As if that last bit of news reassured him in the least.

Josie rocked Davy back and forth. "We need to get the parents' number, see if they know anything..."

"What's that sound?" Miles frowned, looking from Josie to his daughter and back to Josie again. "Do you hear something downstairs?"

Just then, from the lower floor, Ashley called, "Dad?"

He could hardly believe his ears.

"She's back!" exclaimed Hazel, tossing the covers away and leaping from the bed.

Miles was already heading for the door. Josie fell in right behind him.

They all came together in the great room—Miles, Josie and Hazel, in her flannel pajamas. And Ash, looking tired and as sheepish as Miles had ever seen her, a tall, blond-haired boy at her side. The boy held the handle of Ash's big rolling suitcase.

"Dad..." Ash said, her voice so soft and sad it turned his heart to mush.

He went right to her, clasped her shoulders and demanded, "Are you okay?"

"Yeah." Her lower lip quivered. When she swayed toward him with a small cry, he wrapped his arms around her and pulled her close. For a moment that filled him with hope and tenderness, they both held on tight. When she pulled away, her glance went to the woman at his side. "Hey, Josie."

"Ashley." Josie reached out an arm. Ashley moved close for a side hug and a quick peck on Davy's cheek.

Next Ash went to the blond-haired boy. Miles kind of wanted to punch the kid just on principle, but he held himself in check, as his daughter said, "This is Chase. He, um, came and got me when I begged him to. He took me to Heartwood Park. We've mostly just been sitting in his truck for the past four hours while he tried to talk me into coming back home."

After that, well, what could Miles say? "I see." He turned to the boy and offered his hand.

"Uh, good to meet you, Mr. Halstead," said Chase as they shook.

Miles cleared his throat. "Thank you for bringing my daughter home."

The boy gulped and nodded.

Miles didn't even want to punch him anymore.
Which was for the best. He could no longer deny
that Ashley, in fact, did have a boyfriend. At least
she'd found a nice one with a good head on his
shoulders.

And then Chase's phone pinged in his pocket.
He paled a little when he saw who it was. "My
mom. She's freaking and I have some serious ex-
plaining to do."

Ash took his hand. "I'll walk you out."

Miles stifled the urge to order her not to run
off again. He let her go.

The great room was far too silent when the
front door closed. Miles couldn't stand still. He
went and got the coffee started. Hazel asked to
hold Davy. She sat on the couch with him, and
Josie sat beside her.

Five minutes or so crawled by.

Ash came back in. She went straight to the sofa
and sat on Josie's other side.

Miles dropped to one of the chairs and faced
the three females lined up on the couch. "It's been
a rough night for you, Ash. I'll write the note if
you want to be excused from school today."

Ashley shook her head. "I should go. I've got
a chem test I can't miss." Miles kept his mouth
shut, but Ash read his mind. "Okay, Dad. I know
what you're thinking. I probably would've missed

more than a day of school if I'd actually ended up becoming a runaway."

"Yes, you would have. And, all right, you're going to school today. But I want you home right after. Family meeting tonight. We have a lot to talk about."

"Wonderful," said Ash with a groan. "Will I be grounded forever?"

"Not forever…"

She got up and came to him. "Sometimes you really annoy me, Dad."

"I know. Dads are like that." He held out his arms and she let him gather her close. He pressed a kiss to the crown of her head. "I love you, Ash."

"Love you, too, Dad." Too soon, she pulled away and plopped back down next to Josie. Leaning her head on Josie's shoulder, she asked, "Will you be here tonight?"

"I hope so," Josie replied before Miles could say it first. Ashley looked up. She and Josie shared a smile.

An hour later, Ash and Hazel left for school. Davy had fallen asleep by then. Josie put him to bed in the nursery room that had been empty for too many nights now.

When she entered the great room again, Miles patted the space next to him on the sofa. She sat beside him.

"Closer…" He hooked an arm around her. She

scooted right up against him and he nuzzled her velvety cheek. "I've got three words to say to you."

She gave a sweet, low laugh...and pressed two fingers to his mouth. He kissed them. She said, "Alex came to see me yesterday, just for a few hours. You know how she is, always having to get back to Portland and go to work."

"Hold on." He caught her hand. His heart felt like it was lodged in his throat. "Have you changed your mind about wanting those three words, changed your mind about you and me? Is that what you're telling me, Josephine Halstead?"

She put those two fingers to his lips again. "Shh. Don't even think such a thing. I want to hear those words. I want them so bad..."

"But?"

"Well, I was just going to say that Alex lectured me—gently, of course."

"Lectured you? Why?"

"She said you *would* have those words for me, but that I needed to give you time to be ready to say them." She turned her body toward him, drew her knees up on the cushions and hitched an elbow on the backrest. "And I realized she was right."

This wasn't going quite the way he'd imagined it. "Uh. You did?"

"I did. I wasn't as patient as I should have been. My own doubts and fears and bad experiences with love had me pushing you too hard. I see now that giving you an ultimatum is no way to get those three words. So forget them for now. Right now, I really want to come home to you, Miles. I miss you so much."

He couldn't hold back. He reached for her.

She fell into his arms and he kissed her—carefully, at first. Gently. But then her eager response had his control slipping. He gathered her closer and kissed her more deeply. "Josie, thank God," he whispered when he finally lifted away.

A smile trembled across her lips, and she pressed her hand to the side of his face. "I mean it, Miles. I love you and I want to come home."

He tipped up her chin so he could look in those eyes, the ones he wanted to be looking into when they were both old and gray. "Now? Today?"

"Yes."

"Damn. It's good to be this happy." He kissed her again, his whole body relaxing, his soul easing, to hold her close, to have her right here, in his arms that had been aching for her since she moved back to Wild Rose. He could kiss her forever.

But he had so much he needed to say. "My mother came to see me yesterday…" He told her what his mother had said about Fiona…and what Ash had said, too. "I've been a fool, Josie. But not anymore."

"I know that woman broke your heart. It's so wrong, what she did."

"Yeah. I thought I was broken for good, that all I had was my pride, my determination never to let love happen to me again. I was wrong. I just didn't know *how* wrong until I found you. I know you've doubted I could ever get past the mess with Fiona. But I am getting there. Because of you. You're showing me how to put all that hurt behind me. When I look at you, I see real love, Josie. You've taught me that no matter how much of a pigheaded fool a man might be, the right woman is out there, ready to show him how to make his life what he once dreamed it could be."

She sniffled a little and dashed a tear from her eye. "Oh, Miles. I'm so glad. I can't tell you how glad. And Alex was right. I should have been more patient with you."

"You did what you had to do to make me see the light. And now, you're here with me and I never want you to go. Josephine Halstead, I love you. Stay. Please. You're the woman I've dreamed of, the woman I've always been looking for. You're the woman I gave up hope of ever finding. The woman who was right next door the whole time."

"Miles. I love *you*. So much." She lifted her sweet mouth to him.

He pulled her close and kissed her some more, his heart full of gratitude for the life they would share, the future they would build for each other and their children, hand in hand.

And day by day.

"Come on." He stood and pulled her up with him. "This way." And he led her to their bedroom, where they fell across the unmade bed, kissing endlessly as they tore off their clothes.

An hour later, they sat side by side against the headboard in a nest of pillows, laughing, reminding each other how they needed to get up, to go get her things from the cottage at Wild Rose and get going on another busy day…and then laughing some more, holding each other, whispering secrets and making plans.

Just Josie and Miles, in love and together, for now and for the rest of their lives.

* * * * *

Don't miss Alex's story, coming in October 2022, only from Harlequin Special Edition.

And watch for Christine Rimmer's next book, part of the Montana Mavericks continuity, available June 2022!

#2899 CINDERELLA NEXT DOOR
The Fortunes of Texas: The Wedding Gift
by Nancy Robards Thompson

High school teacher and aspiring artist Ginny Sancers knows she is not Draper Fortune's type. Content to admire her fabulous and flirty new neighbor from a distance, she is stunned when he asks her out. Draper is charmed by the sensitive teacher, but when he learns why she doesn't date, he must decide if he can be the man she needs...

#2900 HEIR TO THE RANCH
Dawson Family Ranch • by Melissa Senate

The more Gavin Dawson shirks his new role, the more irate Lily Gold gets. The very pregnant single mom-to-be is determined to make her new boss see the value in his late father's legacy—her livelihood and her home depend on it! But Gavin's plan to ignore his inheritance and Lily—and his growing attraction to her—is proving to be impossible...

#2901 CAPTIVATED BY THE COWGIRL
Match Made in Haven • by Brenda Harlen

Devin Blake is a natural loner, but when rancher Claire Lamontagne makes the first move, he finds himself wondering if he's as content as he thought he was. Is Devin ready to trade his solitary life for a future with the cowgirl tempting him to take a chance on love?

#2902 MORE THAN A TEMPORARY FAMILY
Furever Yours • by Marie Ferrarella

A visit with family was just what Josie Whitaker needed to put her marriage behind her. Horseback-riding lessons were an added bonus. But her instructor, Declan Hoyt, is dealing with his moody teenage niece. The divorced single mom knows just how to help and offers to teach Declan a thing or two about parenting—never expecting a romance to spark with the younger rancher!

#2903 LAST CHANCE ON MOONLIGHT RIDGE
Top Dog Dude Ranch • by Catherine Mann

Their love wasn't in doubt, but fertility issues and money problems have left Hollie and Jacob O'Brien's marriage in shambles. So once the spring wedding season at their Tennessee mountain ranch is over, they'll part ways. Until Jacob is inspired to romance Hollie and her long-buried maternal instincts are revived by four orphaned children visiting the ranch. Will their future together be resurrected, too?

#2904 AN UNEXPECTED COWBOY
Sutton's Place • by Shannon Stacey

Lone-wolf cowboy Irish is no stranger to long, lonely nights. But somehow Mallory Sutton tugs on his heartstrings. The feisty single mom is struggling to balance it all—and challenging Irish's perception of what he has to offer. But will their unexpected connection keep Irish in town...or end in heartbreak for Mallory and her kids?

"You still don't belong here." Mariella crossed her arms
over her chest, and Alex commanded himself not to notice
her body, perfect as it was.

"That makes two of us, and yet here we are."

"I was here first," she muttered. He'd heard the argument
before, but it didn't sway him.

"You're not running me off, Mariella. I needed a fresh
start, and this is the place I've picked for my home."

"My plan was to leave the past behind me. You are a
physical reminder of so many mistakes I've made."

"I can't say that upsets me too much," he lied. It didn't
make sense, but he hated that he made her so uncomfortable.
Hated even more that sometimes he'd purposely drive by

her shop to get a glimpse of her through the picture window. Talk about a glutton for punishment.

She let out a low growl. "You are an infuriating man. Stubborn and callous. I don't even know if you have a heart."

"Funny." He kept his voice steady even as memories flooded him, making his head pound. "That's the rationale Amber gave me for why she cheated with your fiancé. My lack of emotions pushed her into his arms. What was his excuse?"

She looked out at the street for nearly a minute, and Alex wondered if she was even going to answer. He followed her gaze to the park across the street, situated in the center of the town. There were kids at the playground and several families walking dogs on the path that circled the perimeter. Magnolia was the perfect place to raise a family.

If a person had the heart to be that kind of a man—the type who married the woman he loved and set out to be a good husband and father. Alex wasn't cut out for a family, but he liked it in the small coastal town just the same.

"I was too committed to my job," she said suddenly and so quietly he almost missed it.

"Ironic since it was your job that introduced him to Amber."

"Yeah." She made a face. "This is what I'm talking about, Alex. A past I don't want to revisit."

"Then stay away from me, Mariella," he advised. "Because I'm not going anywhere."

"Then maybe I will," she said and walked away.

Don't miss
Wedding Season *by Michelle Major,*
available May 2022 wherever
HQN books and ebooks are sold.

HQNBooks.com

Love Harlequin romance?

DISCOVER.

Be the first to find out about promotions,
news and exclusive content!

f Facebook.com/HarlequinBooks

𝕏 Twitter.com/HarlequinBooks

◎ Instagram.com/HarlequinBooks

℗ Pinterest.com/HarlequinBooks

You Tube YouTube.com/HarlequinBooks

ReaderService.com

EXPLORE.

Sign up for the Harlequin e-newsletter and
download a free book from any series at
TryHarlequin.com

CONNECT.

Join our Harlequin community to
share your thoughts and connect
with other romance readers!
Facebook.com/groups/HarlequinConnection

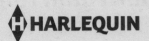

HARLEQUIN

Heartfelt or thrilling, passionate or uplifting—Harlequin is more than just happily-ever-after.

With twelve different series to choose from and new books available every month, you are sure to find stories that will move you, uplift you, inspire and delight you.

SIGN UP FOR THE HARLEQUIN NEWSLETTER
Be the first to hear about great new reads and exciting offers!

Harlequin.com/newsletters